ROGUE ANGEL

KYLIE GILMORE

Cover design by: Michele Catalano Creative

Published by: Extra Fancy Books

ISBN-13: 978-1-947379-26-8

A forbidden love that's meant to be…

1

———

Becca

I have *not* been stood up. I take a quick glance around The Twisted Chord, my favorite bar in Brooklyn, for my date from eLoveMatch. No blond guys wearing a white sweater to be found. It's not that big a place either, just the L-shaped bar and a row of high-top tables across from it. There's a small space for a live band up front. The décor is funky with electric guitars on the walls and fairy lights along the ceiling.

I glance at the empty barstool next to me. Apparently, I have a date with my cardigan. Ha-ha. My purse and white cardigan reserve the seat. *Sigh.*

I check the time on my phone. Eight thirty. The band starts at nine. If he's not here by then, I'll leave. Must. Keep. Positive.

I take a sip of cheap chardonnay, eavesdropping shamelessly on the three guys in their twenties sitting on the other side of my reserved seat. They're similar looking—dark-haired, varying amounts of scruff, with muscular builds filling out T-shirts and faded jeans. I'm guessing they're brothers or cousins. The guy closest to me is the quiet one, but when he speaks, the other two listen intently. He keeps saying they're not going to talk business since it's Friday night, but then he does anyway. He seems intensely into whatever project they're working on, something on the waterfront. Sounds like they're developers. He shifts suddenly, catching my eye, and my breath hitches. His eyes are a piercing blue. I get the strange feeling he can see through me on some deep soul level. My senses go on full alert, my pulse thrumming through my veins.

I face front, embarrassed by my intense reaction to a stranger. It normally takes me a while to warm up to a guy. I'm more on the reserved side. I want to sneak another look at him but don't dare. I don't think I've seen him here before. I'd definitely remember those eyes.

He goes back to his conversation, ignoring me sitting here all alone. I allow myself a quiet sigh of disappointment. Not over him, I assure myself. I'm disappointed that Bill is late. Obviously, I'm not here to pick up some random guy while I'm waiting for my date. I check my phone for a text, missed call, or private message on the dating app. Nothing. My gut does a slow roll.

I square my shoulders and paste a pleasant expression on my face. It's not a big deal to hang solo at a bar on a Friday night. And I may not be solo for long. I mean, yes, Bill is thirty minutes late for our meetup—and I was early, which makes the wait seem longer—but there's still hope. He could've been delayed by work or stuck on the subway or hit by a car. My spirits lift, thinking he's gravely injured somewhere, wishing he could've made it here to meet me. It's not personal at all. He did *not* check me out and bail.

I swear I look just like my dating profile pic—shoulder-length straight light blond hair, pale blue eyes, fair skin, high cheekbones, nose on the larger side. Not a huge nose, but not one of those narrow little things. Sure, I'm tall for a woman at five feet ten, but I don't think that should turn Bill off unless he lied about his height. Some guys are so weird about that. Besides, I've been sitting this whole time and I'm wearing black ballet flats. No way he could tell how tall I am.

I smooth my hair, a teensy worry buzzing through my mind. I've been told I have a cool regal aura (by polite people) and that I'm an ice queen by the not so polite. Which is ridiculous. First of all, I can't help it if I'm a pale color that makes people think "frosty." Second, I'm from a working-class neighborhood in Queens. My parents are both teachers. I'm down to earth and extremely practical. Which is why I know I have to kiss a lot of frogs to find the right partner. I'm twenty-nine and ready to settle down. That's why I've been accepting one date per week for the past seven weeks from eLove-Match, which has the reputation of being the premier service for people seeking serious relationships.

I turn to the front door at the sound of voices, my hopes rising. Nope. It's the band coming in to set up by the front. My shoulders slump, every limb suddenly heavy. I turn back to my wine and take a healthy swallow. Bill seemed so warm and flirty in his texts. I didn't think he'd be a no-show. I'm really getting tired of all these disappointing guys. This is the first time I've been stood up (possibly), but not one single date has progressed to date two. I swear it's not me. We're just not clicking, and I can tell within the first hour. I'm not high maintenance either, despite what my ex claimed. I wouldn't go so far as to say I'm chill—more of a type A go-getter—but I'm really trying to change that and mellow a bit for my own health.

My ex, Oliver, is the one who completely freaked out, not me. I don't think it should've been such a shock that I brought up marriage after a year of dating. It's not like I proposed! I just mentioned that marriage was something I wanted in the near future and wondered if he felt the same way. His answer was to break up with me. Did I mention it was New Year's Eve? Great way to ring in the New Year. Not. I'd like to say I took it in stride, but honestly, it was the beginning of the end. I was already worn down from my management consulting job with its long hours and constant travel and, in my mistaken determination to get over him by putting work first, I spent the next six months sliding right into burnout. I quit at the end of June and gave myself four weeks to recover and find a new direction for my life. I have enough savings, fortunately, to do that. My former job paid extremely well, but it took a serious toll on my health. It's tough to go from a full-throttle career traveling the world to where I am now, finding my way to a new mellower way of life. But I did it. I reprioritized, and everything is going according to plan. Almost.

I peek at my phone, ever hopeful. Finding the right partner is the part of my new life plan that's not working so well. I need to be patient. I'll wait just a little bit longer in case Bill has a legitimate excuse. Anyway, it's been nine months since Oliver and I broke up and I'm over it. Really. Moving on was made immensely easier by Oliver trying to get back together with me a few times "in a casual way." Translation: convenient hookup. Yeah, no, thanks. Not saying it was easy to get over him exactly—my heart is tender—but definitely easier knowing it was a dead end.

A heavy hand lands on my shoulder, jolting me. My date made it here after all! I turn with a bright smile that remains frozen in place as my stomach drops. It's my ex looking tanned and relaxed, his light brown hair artfully mussed. What is Oliver doing here? He hated this place, called it a hole in the wall. He only likes hipster bars with fancy food. And he's brought a woman with him. She's beautiful. *Dammit.* Long dark brown wavy hair, dark eyes with long lashes, busting with curves, and clinging to his arm like he might make a getaway if she doesn't. And me sitting here all alone. This would be a great time for a trapdoor to open and swallow them both. He's got to be here to gloat. Oliver knows this is where I like to hang out. It has everything I need—drinks, good music, and is close to my apartment. Crap. I probably shouldn't have posted a pic on Insta about my fave Friday night hangout last week while waiting for bummer date number six.

Oliver smiles, but it doesn't reach his brown eyes. "How are you, Becca?" His voice drops to a sympathetic tone. "Are you here alone?" He glances over my shoulder, where a couple of women are sitting, chatting animatedly. Why couldn't I have a guy by my side when Oliver decides to make an appearance?

I straighten my spine, determined to brazen this out. "What're you doing here? It's a bit of a hike from the city, isn't it?" He lives in Manhattan. I have the sinking feeling he's here just to show off Miss Curvy to me. I clench my jaw, every muscle tense. I'm not so abundant in the curve department, though they are there. I'm more long and lean. Oliver once asked me why I bother wearing a bra. Asshat.

My gaze collides with piercing-blue-eyes guy, who's just returned from the restroom. His brow furrows slightly like he's trying to suss out the situation. I probably have panic written all over my face. I can't let Oliver think I'm pathetically alone in a bar on a Friday night because I was stood up by a random guy from eLoveMatch. I just can't.

I remove my cardigan and purse from the stool next to me and smile at Mr. Blue Eyes, who's now only a short distance away. "Saved your seat, honey," I say cheerfully, desperately hoping he'll get the message.

The guys he's been sitting with look at me strangely. Sweat trickles down my spine.

Mr. Blue Eyes takes the offered seat—there is a God!—and turns to Oliver. "Hey, I'm Connor. And you are?"

Oliver stiffens. "I'm Oliver, Becca's ex. This is Rose."

Rose bares her teeth in a tight smile. Out of the corner of my eye, I catch the guys Connor was sitting with watching us curiously. *Please don't give me away.*

"Nice to meet ya, Becca's ex and Rose." Connor slips an arm around my shoulders and kisses my temple. My skin flushes hot, my heart thumping hard. I don't know if it's Connor's proximity or the bizarre situation. He smells wonderful, like the ocean and sexy man. He's much bigger than me too—taller with wide shoulders—and I love that I actually feel petite. I've felt statuesque since sixth grade. (Old nickname Lady Liberty after the nearby Statue of Liberty. Kids can be so cruel.)

I glance back at Oliver and say coolly, "Nice to run into you. Have a good night."

Oliver clears his throat. "I dropped by to let you know Rose and I are engaged. I didn't want you to hear it from anyone else. I thought it best to have the conversation face-to-face, given our history."

My eyes narrow. He did come here just to rub it in my face. We don't have any friends in common, so it's not like I would've heard it from someone else. *Hmph.* Back on that fateful New Year's Eve, he first claimed he wasn't ready for marriage, which I accepted, until he added that he couldn't see living with someone *like me* forever. That's when I got a little miffed and gave him a few farewell *dick falling off* wishes.

"He just wanted to be up front with you, considering," Rose adds unhelpfully.

What did Oliver tell her? That *I* was the one who tried to get back together with him multiple times? He's the one who kept texting me for a booty call! At least I thought that's what he meant by getting together in a casual way. Did he just mean a *not getting married but dating* way? Did he miss me like I missed him? And I turned him down flat. Now his ego demands I see what I missed out on.

The happy couple looks at me expectantly.

I swallow hard. They dated for less time than Oliver and I did. I grab Connor's hand and give it a good squeeze before pasting a smile on. "Congrats." I nearly choke on the word. "Why don't you take our seats? Connor and I are just on our way out."

Connor stands and helps me into my cardigan. I owe this guy big time. I grab my purse, thrilled to make my escape.

Connor winks at Oliver. "She can't wait to get me back to her place, as usual."

I laugh. I love that I sound like a fiery passionate woman, despite the fact that passion has proved elusive with my past boyfriends, including Oliver. "That's right."

Connor takes my hand and we walk toward the door. I can feel Oliver's eyes on me.

"Con?" a deep voice calls out. I glance back. It's one of the guys he came here with. My heart races. *So close to the door. Please let me walk out of here with some dignity.*

"Yeah, later," Connor says over his shoulder and walks me out the door.

The moment we step outside, my knees go weak with relief. *Did we really pull it off?*

"Where to?" he asks.

"No idea. Just keep moving. Thank you, by the way." *We did it!* I feel ultra-awake like I just ran a heart-pumping, hurdle-jumping race and won. *Victory! And the crowd goes wild!* Woo! I am *pumped*.

"I could tell he was an ass from a mile away. Don't let that guy ruin your night. There's another bar I like two blocks over with a back garden. Sound good?"

I suddenly realize I'm kinda having a date tonight after all. His hand is warm and calloused holding mine, his walk a slow amble like he's the chill kind of laid-back I've been working so hard to achieve.

"Sure," I chirp nervously. I mean, I don't even know the *basics* I'd normally get from a dating profile—three things he can't live without, the thing he's most passionate about, and the way his friends would describe him. I don't feel right grilling him, though, after he rescued me.

I sneak a sideways glance at him, and my mouth goes dry. He's *gorgeous*. I was too caught up in panic before to fully appreciate his beauty. Thick dark brown hair that's a little long on top, angular cheekbones, a square jaw with just the right amount of scruff. His navy blue T-shirt hugs wide rounded shoulders, a broad chest, and spectacularly formed biceps. A flutter in my belly and a low ache reminds me just how long it's been since I've been with a guy. Too long, as in nine freaking months.

I tear my gaze away, hoping my ogling wasn't too obvious. Insta-lust to this intense degree is new for me, but I'm not going to act on it. That's just not me.

We're about to turn the corner when my eye catches on Oliver and his new fiancée driving off in his candy apple red Porsche. It's ridiculous to have a car when you live in the city. I used to think that car was a sign of his success, but now all I see is another ego booster. Oliver and I were both obsessed with chasing success, and maybe that's why we worked as a couple for a while. I'm glad I got off the success train because there's just no stop where you feel like you've reached the satisfying end. It just keeps going round and round in an endless cycle of work, work, work.

Connor stops me and pulls his phone from his back jeans pocket. "Just let me text my brothers. They're probably wondering what the hell that was back there."

"Actually, my ex just left, so if you want to hang with them, I don't mind. It sounded like you had a lot to talk about."

His intense blue eyes lock on mine as he says flatly, "I'm no longer useful to you."

Oh no, I've insulted him. I put a hand on his arm, immediately contrite. His arm is like warm marble, all sculpted muscle. I lick my lips and try to come up with something reassuring to keep him from taking offense. I need to stop touching him to think. "It's not that at all. I so appreciate you coming to my rescue. My ex just wanted to rub his new fiancée in my face after breaking up with me over his inability to commit. I'd love to have a drink, but I don't want you to feel obligated. You were already having your own evening."

One corner of his mouth curves up. My fingers tingle with the sudden urge to touch his scruffy jaw. "So let's go back to The Twisted Chord for a drink."

I smile. "Sure. I like the live music."

He's quiet as we walk back, and that just makes me feel the need to fill the silence.

"Thanks again for coming to my rescue," I say.

"Happy to. I wanted to meet you, but I thought you were waiting for a date since you saved a seat with your stuff."

My cheeks flame. So much for making a good impression. First, it's obvious from my ex that I have terrible taste in men, and second, it's clear I was stood up.

"My friend got held up at work," I lie. "No date."

He inclines his head.

"I haven't seen you at The Twisted Chord before," I say.

"Yeah, I usually go to a bar in my old neighborhood, but this is my new place since I moved."

"Oh. So that means I'll probably see you there regularly." A surge of adrenaline goes through me at the thought, my pulse racing, all of my senses heightened. *Be cool!* I've never had this intense a reaction to a guy I just met. I can't let it show.

"Depends. I'm not into the bar scene so much anymore. I went more for my brothers."

I want to ask what he's into and how he meets people. Maybe he uses a dating app like I do. That all feels too personal, so I keep my mouth shut.

We arrive at The Twisted Chord's entrance and Connor opens the door for me. A simple gesture that makes every nerve ending tingle to awareness, the butterflies dancing in my belly. I kinda have a thing for good manners.

He smiles down at me as I brush by him, and I'm so enthralled with his sexy clean scent and the way his smile lights up his face that I can't look away.

Bam! I fall sideways through the doorway, dropping like a rock to the tile floor. *Ow, ow, ow.* I forgot about the step. The bar gets quiet, every eye in the place on me. I just lie there on my side for a moment, my face hot, my hip stinging. Mostly it's my ego that's bruised. Would it be so terrible for me to actually look good in front of this guy?

Connor leans over me. "Break anything?"

"No." I start to get up when he scoops me off the floor, cradled in his arms, and carries me to a cozy table for two in the back corner.

I still feel every eye in the place on me, but my eyes are only for my hero. Connor *last name unknown*. A prince among men.

$$2$$

Connor

I take in the pink-cheeked flustered woman sitting across from me. Becca is strikingly beautiful. Her red lips in contrast to her fair looks caught my eye earlier. She's tall for a woman with slim long legs. She's also having a helluva night that I hope I can salvage. I don't think I've ever felt this drawn to a woman before. "I'm gonna get us some drinks and let my brothers know what's up. Don't fall out of your chair while I'm gone."

She scowls, pursing her lush red lips. "I'm not normally clumsy. I took ballet for years." She doesn't sound like she's from Brooklyn. I can't tell where she's from. She has no recognizable accent at all.

In any case, I'm not sure what ballet has to do with falling through an open doorway, so I let that slide. "More white wine?" *See how I noticed what you were drinking earlier?*

Her brows lift. "Yes. Chardonnay, please."

I head back to the bar and place the order before shifting over to my brothers, Brendan and Garrett. Funny, Garrett recently shaved and Brendan's beard needs a trim. Together they'd have the perfect level of scruff like me. We're like the three bears—too furry, too spare, just right. Proof being Goldilocks chose me. Ha.

I stick to the most important thing. "I met someone, so I'll see ya later. We'll talk shop on the drive to the waterfront Monday morning."

"Yup, saw ya come to her rescue in the ol' fake-boyfriend maneuver," Brendan says, taking a pull on his beer and casually glancing around the bar, probably looking for a woman. He favors redheads on some wacky theory that they're more fiery.

Garrett leans around Brendan, offering me a fist bump, his aquamarine eyes twinkling with his smile. "She looks like she stepped out of an ad for a luxury car. Real classy." He's the only one of us who got our dad's eye color, which is supposed to indicate a true ruler of Villroy since the Rourke eye color matches the sea there. Not that the youngest son of the exiled family could ever be king. Did I mention we're descended from royalty? The rest of us got our mom's blue eyes, showing our commoner blood.

I incline my head at Garrett. We call him Beast on account of his huge muscles. He's right. Becca does look classy. She's in a crisp white blouse with black trousers, perfectly made up, not a hair out of place, even after her tumble through the doorway. She dresses and sounds like a corporate professional yet she's hanging in a funky neighborhood bar in Brooklyn. I would've pegged her for a Manhattan high-end cocktail lounge kind of person, sipping on a thirty-buck martini. The drinks here are cheap. The contradictions in her intrigue me. Maybe because my whole life has been a bizarre contradiction too—I'm a prince raised in Brooklyn with none of the wealth or privilege that goes with the title. It would've been easier not to know what I was missing out on, but Dad never let us forget we had royal blood. Not that I'm bitter. I like my life here in Brooklyn, and our family is tight.

Brendan jerks his chin at me. "A classy woman likes *you*? What'd you say to her?" We always give each other shit— Rourke brother credo—but we also have each other's backs, so it balances out.

I smirk. "So you admit you need pickup advice from your

big brother." I'm only two years older, but I've got to claim authority.

He socks me on the shoulder. "Please. I've got zero problem picking up women. I'll pick one up tonight."

The band starts playing a loud cover of Aerosmith's "Walk this Way." Just as well I can't hear Brendan's impassioned defense of his "sophisticated" moves. Not my concern.

I glance over to the table and catch Becca staring at me. She's into me. And I'm glad she was stood up tonight. Yeah, I could tell she was lying. I can read people, and with her it's not hard at all. Watching her at the bar earlier, she went from nervous to anxious to resigned over the course of the forty-five minutes I saw her. Then she was agitated with her ex, and then when she tripped, embarrassed, and now? Well, now she looks like she's anticipating something exciting, and that something is me.

A few minutes later, I return to the table with the drinks. She gives me a small smile and pitches her voice over the music. "Thanks! Do you like live music?"

I drag my chair to the side of the table so we're close enough to hear each other. "Yeah, it's okay."

Her cheeks flush bright pink. "I love it *mumble, mumble.*" She's on the shy side. I don't mind that. I'm not a big talker and I find chatty people tiring.

I lean close, tilting my ear toward her. "Say again."

"I said my dad is a music teacher, so I grew up with music."

"Cool." I take a pull on my beer. "My dad worked in accounting for my uncle's construction company. Now he's in real estate, so you could say I grew up with buildings."

She laughs, a musical sound I want to hear more of. I smile. *So far, so good.* I leave out that my dad abdicated the throne to Villroy to marry my mom. It's a complicated history between the current ruling family and mine. I don't like that we're considered the riffraff of the family by many of the older generation. Though, according to my brothers, I should really be playing the prince card more. Apparently, a lot of women have a prince fantasy.

She leans close to speak directly in my ear, and I breathe in the delicious scent of citrus, spice, and something uniquely her. My mouth actually waters. "Is your dad involved in waterfront real estate?"

I shift to meet her eyes, and we're suddenly extremely close. Her pale blue eyes dilate, her red lips parting. "You were listening to our conversation earlier?"

She looks away, pink tingeing her cheeks. "I couldn't help but hear."

"What?" I say, cupping my hand by my ear. Mostly because I want her close again.

She obliges. "Sorry. I couldn't help but overhear. Before the band started playing, it was so quiet in here."

"Who were you supposed to meet up with?"

She doesn't reply, leaning back and sipping her wine.

I lean in. "You must've been waiting on a date."

Her eyes widen. "Why do you say that?"

I gesture to her outfit. "You're dressed too nice for this place."

She glances down at herself. "This is casual." She holds up her wrist. "See, I even accessorized with a simple bracelet. Plus I'm wearing ballet flats."

"Ah." I imagine she would normally wear a formal dress if this is casual to her.

"What?" she asks, looking suddenly self-conscious.

I shake my head. "Nothing."

The band launches into another rock song, this one unrecognizable. Maybe one of their own.

I lean close and whisper in her ear, "I was just asking about your date to find out if you're single. Were you waiting on a guy?"

She looks away, biting her lower lip like maybe she's trying to decide how to play this. I just want her to be straight with me. Maybe I misread the situation, and she sees me more as a rescuer from her asshole ex and not actually the kind of guy she's interested in. "No hard feelings either way. Just tell me."

She leans in and whispers, "I was supposed to meet

someone here, someone new, not a boyfriend. Anyway, he was a no-show, which is a really crappy thing to do."

She's single. I'm in.

"That sucks," I say. *For that guy.*

She smiles sorta forlornly. "I waited too long for him. I should've just went home, made some popcorn, and watched the Home Improvement channel. I like when they take a dud house and renovate it."

I smile. "Sounds like the perfect night."

She smiles back, her pale blue eyes sparkling. "This is better."

I lean close. "Yeah?"

"Yeah." She sips her wine, trying to look casual, but still looking pink and flustered. "Do you like the Home Improvement channel?"

"I'm the guy you watch on the Home Improvement channel."

She sets her drink down, her eyes wide. "You're on TV?"

"Ha! No. I build and renovate, commercial and residential. I work for my family's construction business."

Her gaze drops to my bicep and then roams over my chest. "No wonder you're so, uh, fit."

"Yeah, thanks." I hide a smile by taking a sip of beer. "Where're you from?"

"Originally?"

"Yeah, originally. You don't sound like you're from around here."

She leans in, whispering, "I hope this doesn't sound like I'm down on local accents—yours is clearly from Brooklyn—but I worked with a voice coach to lose my Queens accent. It's just that at work people associated it with being uneducated, even though it has nothing to do with education. It's just perception, and I needed to be taken seriously at my job."

I stare at her. "Get out. You're from Queens?"

"I sawr it with my own eyes! It was right heyah!" she exclaims, throwing an extra *R* into "saw" like God intended. She left the *R* out of "here," naturally. Some people make fun of the New Yawk accent, but I think it's awesome. I know a native New Yorker anywhere, Becca being the exception with her fancy voice coach.

I grin. "Sounds perfectly normal to me. Bit shriller than us laid-back Brooklynites."

"Hey, I'm a Brooklynite too. I've lived here six years now, though mostly I traveled for work."

"What do you do?"

"I used to do consulting. Now I'm recalibrating."

I lean close. *God, she smells good.* "And what's that, recalibrating?"

"You know, having a do-over."

"Not sure what you mean, but okay."

She exhales sharply. "Basically, I stayed up all night questioning every single part of my life and what the hell I wanted, and came up with a plan to rejigger everything."

"Like a life renovation."

"Exactly!"

"How's it going so far?"

She stares at my mouth. "Better by the moment."

I slowly move in, wanting a kiss but not sure if it's too forward. I hover close for a hot second and glance at her eyes. They're closed. *That's a go.* And then she surprises me, kissing me first. A rush of lust hits me hard.

She pulls back, staring deeply into my eyes. She felt it too. I hold her gaze, the air rife with tension. It's been a long time since a simple kiss made me feel like this—awake, alive, eager for more. I see the moment she decides to go for it, her lashes fluttering down as she kisses me again. Her lips are soft and pliant under mine. I'm about to deepen the kiss when I hear a masculine voice next to us.

"Hey, I'm Brendan." My idiot brother. *Dammit.*

I turn and glare at him, but he's too busy giving Becca his most charming smile to notice. Garrett stands behind him, looking toward the front door like he didn't want to come over here. He's got better survival instincts.

"What?" I bark.

Brendan gestures toward my mouth. "That color complements your skin tone." I must have Becca's red lipstick on me.

I wipe with a napkin and crumple it up. I debate insults over his untrimmed beard. *Are you trying to go full Viking? Did a ferret die on your face?* But then he moves closer to Becca, and I go on alert.

He pitches his voice to be heard over the music. "We're on our way out, but I wanted to put in a good word for Con here. I'm his brother, so I know the real deal."

Becca's eyes dance with amusement as she looks between me and my irritating brother. "And the real deal is what?"

"Get outta here, man," I say, giving him a shove.

He laughs. "He actually has women friends."

I shake my head. "I have one woman friend." I turn to Becca. "We grew up together. Now she's married with twin girls, living out on Long Island."

Brendan leans down between us. "It still counts."

Becca's brows lift. "What exactly does it mean to have a woman friend on Long Island?"

I shrug. It means my brother is making a nuisance of himself.

Brendan smiles widely. He's either about to do me a huge favor and actually make me look good or kill my chances with Becca entirely. "It means he's capable of relating to women on a nonphysical level. That's a plus, right? It means he's evolved."

He's going to get me stuck in the friend zone with that comment! I don't want Becca on a nonphysical level.

"Or it could mean you're still a Neanderthal," I growl.

He feigns indignation, his blue eyes wide. "Hey, no need to bring me into it." He grins at Becca. "Are ya into the Neanderthal thing?"

She laughs.

"You can leave now," I tell him.

He lifts his palms. "I will, I will." He leans toward Becca. "Seriously, though, just because he never lasted more than a couple of months in a relationship doesn't mean he couldn't. He's got real potential."

Becca looks like she's trying not to laugh. This is so embarrassing.

I groan and scrub a hand over my face. "Seriously, you're not helping."

He shoots me an aggrieved look. "I am so helping. She looks like a relationship kind of girl."

"Shut up," I snap. It's like he's trying to ruin everything before I've gotten anywhere with her. He's pouring cement around my feet in the friend zone—nonphysical, has women friends, could stick around. *He's the guy friend you always wanted.*

"He's not wrong," Becca says.

I glare at Brendan. "He's wrong just by being here."

He musses my hair, and I smack his hand away. "Am I cramping your style?" He grins at me and turns to Becca. "Kidding. He's got no game."

Fuck you, I do have game. I keep the words to myself because I'm not sure Becca would like hearing how my game helps me pick up women easily whenever I want. Instead, I glare my best *I'm gonna kick your ass* glare at him. "I swear—"

"Alright, I'm going." He backs away. "Come on, Beast."

Garrett lifts a hand to us before following Brendan out the door. They're roommates now. I recently got my own place after living with Brendan for a while. Garrett used to be with a bunch of guys in a condo owned by one of his friends' parents. That place got sold and they scattered.

"Beast?" Becca asks once they're out the door.

"He works out too much, overly muscled beast." I take a pull on my beer, trying to calm down. I know my brothers and I give each other shit, but this is not the time.

She gives me a small sweet smile. "He did fill out his T-shirt nicely. I think his boobs are bigger than mine though."

We crack up.

"I'm sure yours are more fun," I say.

"Wanna find out?"

I'm about to say *sure* when she slaps a hand over her mouth, her eyes wide.

She drops her hand. "I can't believe I just said that."

I wink. "I don't mind."

"Let's just listen to the music."

So we do. I play it cool, occasionally talking to her about music she likes while touching her arm and then her hand. I need to touch her. She's part shy, part confident, all sexy woman.

The band finishes at eleven, and it's weirdly quiet with just the conversation of the people at the bar and a few of the tables.

She gives me a bright smile for no reason, which makes me think she's about to say goodbye. I brace myself. I don't want to say goodbye just yet, but I'm not going to push where I'm not wanted. "Well, Connor, this has been a very nice evening."

She sounds formal, too polite. We're past that after all our close conversation and that amazing kiss. I take her hand and brush my thumb over the inside of her wrist. I meet her eyes and lower my voice to the husky tone women love. At least they do if they're into me. "I had a good time too."

She stares at my thumb caressing her wrist. I glance down. She's got goose bumps on her pale skin. A good sign.

Our gazes collide, and I want to kiss her so bad I can't hold back. I give her a soft kiss, nothing too aggressive. I want her to meet me halfway.

Her voice comes out breathy. "I never do this, but do you want to walk me home?"

"Sure."

I stand and take her hand, walking her out the door, making sure she takes the step down outside without incident.

She stops on the sidewalk. "I didn't mean that, actually."

"Oh. Okay." Guess she changed her mind about me walking her home. Sucks for me, but what can you do? Maybe I can get her number.

She steps closer. "I meant, do you want to go home with me?" She grimaces, her cheeks dotted with pink. "Oh God, I never move this fast. It's just—"

"Yes."

3

Becca

I can't believe I'm doing this. I'm walking hand in hand with a sexy guy straight out of one of my builder renovation fantasies—hey, those home renovation shows can be very inspiring to single ladies—and we're going back to my place. Me with Hot Builder Guy! I never move this quickly. I have a strict five-date rule before I invite a guy to my place so I'm sure he's interested in more than just my body. Gah! I'm such a hypocrite because now *I'm* the one who's so turned on by his body. His brother's muscles practically burst out of his shirt, but Connor's are better, perfectly filling out his blue T-shirt. This man is not a gym rat. He's earned those muscles. Don't even get me started on the way he fills out his jeans. And his hands are so nice too, warm and calloused from his work.

And that kiss! An explosion of sparks racing over my skin, a flash of heat, and a pull for more like I've never felt before.

I sneak another sideways glance at him and then linger. *Mmm-hmm, hello, Hot Builder Guy.* For once I'm not worried the sex will be a huge disappointment. He's all laid-back confidence. And you know what? I deserve to have a little fun. It's been almost a year since I've been with a man. Okay, nine months, but it sure feels like a year.

I lift my gaze to his profile, checking his expression—he seems perfectly relaxed and fine with everything. I'm pretty sure he's a good guy. He works with his brothers and is close enough with them to hang at a bar together. He bought me a drink, asked me questions about myself (instead of just bragging about himself like most guys), and last but not least, he *carried* me when I crash-landed on the floor. No man has *ever* carried me. I don't know if it's my height or my demeanor, but guys just don't see me as the cutesy carrying type. All of that is enough to legitimately say this is a guy I like for more than just his body. My guilt eases, making me feel instantly lighter. Yes. There's definitely potential for more than one night with Hot Builder Guy. Therefore, in conclusion, ipso facto—deep breath—it's perfectly okay to enjoy a wild passionate night with him right away. I did have a goal to let loose a little more and expand my comfort zone. It's all in my life plan.

"Your eyes are burning a hole in me," he says in a teasing voice. "Anything you wanna talk about, or you're just enjoying the view?"

Busted! I fight a blush. Hopefully he can't see it in the dim glow of the streetlights. "I was just, uh, trying to remember if I had anything to offer you to drink."

"I don't need a drink."

"I definitely have water."

He grins. "I do enjoy a fine glass of water. Hope it's a good vintage."

I laugh. And then I get quiet. There's nothing more I can add to the conversation that won't reveal more than I want him to know. Like how much I want him and how far this is from my comfort zone. Truth is, I've been turned on ever since he leaned close and spoke in that sexy deep voice right in my ear. He smells so good. Like the ocean but also warm and sensual. Can a guy smell like that? Maybe it's the testosterone pouring off him in waves. It's enough to make any woman woozy with lust.

I glance up at him, and he smiles, giving my hand a reassuring squeeze. It's a genuine smile, reaching his stunning blue eyes, which are sparkling down at me like he's thrilled to be with me. Or maybe that's just the streetlight reflecting off them. Who cares? I choose to believe he's thrilled.

"This is my place," I say, gesturing to the six-story brick building at the end of the block. "It's a prewar building, so my apartment has a lot of cute charming stuff like arched entryways and a built-in set of bookshelves. They just renovated the kitchen before I moved in, so that's modern. The lobby is gorgeous too—white post and beam ceiling, inlaid wood paneling on the walls, marble tiled floor." I almost say that we don't have to worry about being too loud because of the thick plaster walls and concrete floors in the building, but decide it's a little too on the nose.

"Sounds like you watch a lot of the Home Improvement channel. Or are you about to convince me to sign a lease on an apartment here? Is this a real estate hustle?"

I laugh a little. "No hustle." I'm babbling because we're almost at my building and I never do this and I don't even know *how* to do this. I mean, obviously, I know how to have sex. I'm not a virgin. I just don't know how to initiate the much-desired wild passionate night without being awkward. I did trip walking through a doorway because he was so close and smelled amazing.

This is what it means to step out of your comfort zone. Just be cool like him.

I pick up the pace, figuring the faster we get to my apartment, the less chance of me babbling more inane facts about my building.

As soon as we enter the lobby, Connor exclaims, "Look at that post and beam construction! Very nice example of a prewar building." He winks.

My cheeks burn, my mouth flapping open and then closed. I've got no witty comeback. Just as I'm convinced he sees me as a total dork, he wraps an arm around my shoulders, giving me a squeeze before walking with me to the elevator. *Okay, relax. He's just teasing. Obviously he's not overthinking things and worrying I only want him for his sexy body.*

"Prewar building with an elevator," he says, pushing the button. "Nice."

"I thought so."

We step into the elevator, which is small and dim. I hit the button for my floor. Six.

"Top floor," he says, arching his brows over twinkling eyes. "Fancy."

The elevator makes its way up, cranking like it's on its last legs.

I relax a little. "It has high ceilings, too, with parquet wooden floors."

He gives me a sexy smile, wrapping an arm around my waist and pulling me close so we're nose to nose, chest to chest. I flush hot from head to toe. "Talk more construction to me."

I stare at his chest, embarrassed. "I'm probably boring you. You live and breathe this stuff."

He strokes my hair back from my face and then grazes his fingers along the line of my jaw before tipping my face up to his. "I do, but I like hearing you so jazzed about it."

My stomach dips. I feel like I'm on the edge of a cliff, about to take a freefall dive into the unknown. It's the intense look in his eyes. My mouth goes dry. "This elevator is ancient."

"Uh-huh. I'm gonna kiss you now."

I immediately close my eyes. "Ready."

I feel his laugh rumble through his chest as much as hear it before he finally makes contact, his lips brushing over mine. Once, twice. I nearly sigh in blissful happiness until he pulls away.

That's it? I grab the front of his shirt and pull him back. "Hey, I wasn't done."

"You weren't?" he asks with what I can only assume is mock surprise. I'm not sure, though, since I barely know the guy. *Oh God, I barely know this guy!*

His large hand cradles my jaw, and then his mouth covers mine, promptly silencing my inner voice. His sexy scent surrounds me. His lips are *glorious.* I want to climb him like a studly sex pole. Time stops as I revel in the thrill of finding a wonderful kisser. This bodes so well for the bedroom.

The elevator halts with a jerk, and we come up for air. *We're here. Yes!*

I grab his hand and stride purposefully down the hall to my corner apartment. I get my key from my purse, stick it in the lock, and fumble opening the door because he's kissing a trail of hot kisses down the side of my neck. Finally, I'm in. He follows me, the door shutting quietly behind him. I shove my keys in my purse and toss it on the small table by the door.

I turn to him, eager for more.

His piercing blue eyes meet mine. Why does it feel like he can see right through me? Does he sense I'm both excited and a little nervous? Is he waiting to follow my lead?

The fantastic elevator kiss just moments ago gives me the confidence to be bold. I wrap my arms around his neck and kiss him passionately. He returns the kiss with equal enthusiasm. *Yes!* I melt against him, my limbs heavy, a delicious heat flooding me. Desire pools low in my belly. The kiss goes on and on. The urge to get as close as physically possible overwhelms me. His big hands rest on my hips, and I suddenly need more.

I tear my mouth away, breathing hard. "I want you."

One corner of his mouth lifts, his blue eyes sparkling. "I got that much when you wrapped your leg around me and thrust repeatedly, but it's nice to hear."

My leg is up high around his hip. I may have been grinding against him. Before I can lower my leg, he gives me a boost so both my legs are wrapped around his waist. Our mouths collide in a frenzied kiss, the heat raging between us. He's pressing against me in just the right spot, and then it gets even better. He turns and pins me against the wall, his mouth devouring mine as he grinds into me. It's so intense, so...oh, oh, oh. *Don't stop, don't stop.* It's an endless kiss, and I'm climbing higher and higher on my private elevator to the penthouse suite of glittery starbursts of pleasure. My body jerks hard as an explosion of white-hot pleasure steals my breath, rushing through my core and radiating outward. Oh my God.

He lifts his head. "Did you just—"

"Yes!" I beam and kiss him soundly on the mouth. "It's been way too long."

He starts walking down the hall with me still plastered against his front.

"Wonderful man." I heap on the praise as I stroke his heated shoulders and back. "Wonderful, wonderful man."

He smiles as he steps into my bedroom and flips the light switch, which gives a soft glow from the overhead fixture onto light wood furniture with white accents. I'm so glad I sprang for the king-sized bed because now I've got a big man to fill the space. And to fill me. I throb in anticipation.

"You're wonderful too," he says, pulling back the white down blanket and lowering me to the mattress. "And beautiful."

He kisses me again, and I pull at his T-shirt, frustrated by all the clothes between us. He leans back and takes off his T-shirt in one smooth two-handed move. I sit up, eager to feel all that gorgeous muscle, and then we're kissing and ripping at each other's clothes.

It's hot.

It's wild.

It's *everything*.

I break the kiss just long enough to grab a condom from the nightstand because I'm never unprepared, and then we're back on track. He covers me, fitting himself between my legs, and our gazes collide for a charged moment. My breath hitches at the smoldering look in his eyes.

He strokes my hair back from my face before cradling my jaw. The tender gesture undoes me. My throat tightens unexpectedly, my eyes hot.

He kisses me gently. "Ready?"

"Yes," I manage through the tightness in my throat.

He thrusts inside me in one smooth stroke, and we both moan. I ache in the most delicious way, my body straining to accommodate him. It's been so freaking long. He stills and frames my face with both hands, kissing me deeply. It's more than good. It's bliss, like the merging of body and soul. I spear my fingers through his thick hair and then roam my palms all over the hard planes of his muscular heated back. I need to get closer still. I wrap my legs high around him, taking him as deeply as I can. He groans into my mouth.

He lifts his head, gazing into my eyes. "Becca."

"More," I demand.

He nips my lower lip, jolting me, before pumping in hard thrusts, not too fast, not too slow, so-o-o good. On and on and on, his breath harsh by my ear. I close my eyes, lost in a haze of pleasure.

"Yes, yes, yes," I say, nearly incoherent. It's never been this good before.

He kisses along my jaw and then sucks the cord of my neck. Pleasure spears through me as an orgasm hits unexpectedly, rocking me helplessly against him. He groans into my neck, pumping hard and fast for his own release, bringing more and more pleasure, before letting go with a harsh sound. He gives me his weight, almost like a hug, and I smile to myself. A surge of affection has me hugging him tight.

Holy crap. Two orgasms in one night! Unprecedented! And they were much better than what I achieve solo. What a wonderful man. Suddenly I have this craving. It's like he awakened the orgasm monster and she's hungry for more.

I stroke his back, enjoying the shape and feel of all that spectacular heated muscle. "Question."

"Yeah?" The word is hot against my neck. Did I wear him out? Is he too tired to lift his head?

I can't help myself. *I need, I need, I need.* "Can I convince you to stay long enough for another orgasm? I know you were already so generous with the first two, but it's sort of made me want more."

He lifts his head, a wide smile spreading across his gorgeous face. "Greedy, are we?"

"It's just that it's been so long."

He kisses me. "You don't need a reason. Yes. I will give

you more. Later." He rolls off me and finds his way to the bathroom.

I throw my arms to my sides and stretch languorously. Amazing sex, amazing orgasms. I'm so damn lucky I found this guy. Hot Builder Guy. Connor somebody. I should find out his last name. Later. I'm so relaxed and sleepy now.

A few moments later, he turns off the light and gets into bed, shifting me so he can spoon me from behind. I am in heaven. It's been so long since I've been held.

He strokes my hair back and whispers, "I'm beat from work today. We did a lot of demo. Let me sleep a bit and then I'm at your service."

"No problem. I'm tired too." What a fantastic turnaround for my night. First I was stood up by some random guy from a dating app, and now I've had two orgasms *and* I'm getting held with a promise of more orgasms to come. A bubble of pure happiness spreads through me, making my entire body relax in contentment. "I should know your name."

He nips my shoulder, and I squeak in surprise. "You forgot my name and you still demand more orgasms?"

I can hear the smile in his voice. "I know it's Connor, but what's your last name?"

"No last name. I'm like Beyoncé. Scratch that. What's the guy version?"

"Elvis? Bono? Prince?"

"Yeah, I'm like Prince." He grinds his hips into me like he's doing a sexy Prince move.

I fall asleep with a smile on my face.

I wake on the verge of orgasm and realize I was in the throes of my usual hot builder dream from my favorite home renovation show, *Reno Magic,* only this time instead of host Clint Owens, it was me and Connor *last name unknown.*

I roll over to find him sleeping on his back. I don't know what time it is, but it's still dark outside. I can just barely make out his features in the glow from the streetlight peeking in the edges of the window shades. "Con, are you awake?" I whisper loudly. "I want you again."

He mumbles something unintelligible in his sleep, so I

content myself with a slow slide of the covers down his naked body just to admire him for a bit. Not only does he have defined pecs and six-pack abs, there's a deep V at his waist. His cock is impressive, even at rest, his thighs thick and muscular. I don't think I've ever been with such a gorgeous man. I look up at his face. Still sleeping. I decide it would be okay to kiss his scruffy jaw, so I do. He still smells amazing— like the ocean, warm sunshine, and a breeze of Hot Builder Guy sex appeal. What is that scent? I don't know if it's cologne or just him, but I love it. I kiss gently along his neck, breathing him in greedily, and then explore lower to his chest. I drop a kiss on his abs, which are crazy beautiful with muscular ridges, and then I lie next to him, watching him sleep so peacefully. Beautiful, sexy man.

I can't help myself. I need him awake. Maybe another kiss will do it. I hover over him, planting my hands on either side of his shoulders, careful not to rest my weight against him, and kiss him gently on the lips.

He doesn't stir.

I sigh. I should leave him alone. He did say he was tired from doing demo work today. I admire his powerful-looking shoulders and biceps, imagining him at work shirtless, swinging a sledgehammer, taking out drywall and wooden beams, wiping the sweat from his brow. Oh God. Now there's an ache low in my belly *and* a throbbing pulse between my legs. I've never wanted like this before. Just one more kiss, and I'll let him sleep. A goodnight kiss.

I press my lips softly to his. "Ahhh!" I shriek at the top of my lungs. He just flipped me over!

His forearms are anchored on the mattress, holding his weight as he grins down at me. "You woke the beast."

My heart thunders against my rib cage, my breath coming hard. I attempt to play it cool. "I thought Beast was your brother."

"You let me know." He kisses gently, slowly along the column of my neck, tasting, occasionally scraping his teeth against me, drawing a hot shiver. The adrenaline leaves my body, replaced by a heightened pleasure, all of my nerve endings tingling as he continues kissing his way down my body. He caresses my breasts, kissing and suckling each one, lavishing attention on them. This man. I melt into the mattress, moaning softly. Hot tingles race down my body as he goes lower still, kissing a trail down my stomach, further, further. My breath hitches, my hips lifting in anticipation.

"Wonderful man!" I exclaim as he makes contact with pleasure central.

He nuzzles into my inner thigh.

"Why'd you stop?" I demand.

"Wonderful man," he says, and I hear the smile in his voice. "You're very enthusiastic."

"Please don't stop."

He obliges, dipping his head between my legs, and proceeding to blow my mind. His lips, his tongue. My God. I bite my lower lip to keep from blurting anything else out that might put an end to the intense pleasure. My fingers clutch the sheets, and then I'm chanting his name like it's the only way to keep this going, faster and faster. *Con, Con, Con. Come, come, come.* My breath hitches, and I'm *gone*. Wave after wave of pleasure crashes over me in an overwhelming rush. He stays with me, pushing me on relentlessly as I rock against him, lost in never-ending pleasure.

Finally I collapse, and he shifts away. I'm dead. A blissful satisfied kind of dead.

And when I'm finally able to move again, he's ready for me, condom on. I climb on top of him and ride him with wild abandon.

I never want it to end.

Neither does he because we're all over each other the rest of the night.

Until at some point we collapse in exhaustion, ending the best night of my life.

4

Becca

I wake to a cold bed, the bright morning sun peeking in around the window shades, and the sound of rustling clothes nearby. I pry an eye open to find Connor getting dressed with his back to me. I peer at the nightstand. It's seven a.m. on Saturday morning. My gut tightens. This isn't what I thought after all. I swallow hard. I thought there might've been potential for more between us. Obviously it was just one hot night. He's sneaking out practically at the crack of dawn on a Saturday. This sucks. In the harsh light of day, I feel awful that it was just sex. I mean, yes, I enjoyed it A LOT, but I guess part of me sorta hoped it was the start of something.

I screwed up. *Duh.* Going to bed with a guy I just met is obviously sending the signal that it's temporary. He probably thinks I do this all the time. Hell, *he* probably does this all the time. I veered from the life plan and this is what happens. Twenty-nine, ready to settle down, yet I stupidly do this. Just because of my hot builder fantasy and lack of sex. I have to do better.

I roll to my side away from him, closing my eyes. I don't want to watch him go. To think at the beginning of the night I was feeling so guilty believing I might be taking advantage of him with all my lusting for his sexy body when it was actually the other way around. At least *I* took the time to think of his other qualities.

I hear him moving around the bed toward me and deepen my breathing so he thinks I'm sleeping. I know, I know, but it's just that I've never had to deal with the morning after a one-night stand. That's exactly why I have a five-date rule before sex. To eliminate the possibility of any of this awkwardness.

The mattress dips as he sits next to me. He smooths my hair back over my ear. "Too bad you're sleeping because I was gonna offer you a goodbye orgasm."

My eyes fly open. "What?" *Is it bad that I want that?*

He laughs, his blue eyes twinkling. "I knew you were faking sleep. I've got five brothers always trying to pull one over on each other. I don't fall for much."

I roll to my back. "I was just really tired." *And embarrassed.*

He holds my jaw as he leans down and kisses my heated cheek. "I don't know anyone who blushes in their sleep." He straightens and pulls his phone from his back pocket. "What's your number?"

My eyes widen. "You want my number?"

"Why do you sound so surprised?"

I stare at the ceiling, blinking a few times as my mind tries to rearrange my previous take on the situation. Did he think of my other qualities too?

"Becca?"

"I thought it was a onetime thing," I blurt. Not that I want it to be, but I'm confused, very tired, and way out of my element. Casual hot sex guy is now wanting more. But more what? Is he going to text me every time he wants a hookup, or is this something else?

He cocks his head, studying me. "Maybe it could be two times."

"Two times," I echo. That sounds casual. I should say no because it's obviously not going anywhere, but then there's the multiple-orgasm situation to consider too. I can't completely discount that.

"Yeah, or whatever. Number, please."

I give it to him without a second thought because he was so polite. It's my habit to reward manners because I appreciate them.

He smiles, tucks his phone in his pocket, and leans down to me. I'm expecting a quick peck but instead he gently kisses my forehead, the end of my nose, and then my lips. "Later, Becca."

"Bye, later," I mutter, a little stunned by the unexpected turn of events.

He strides from the room. I listen to the front door quietly closing behind him.

What just happened?

He was kinda sweet and tender at the end there. I review our conversation, searching for clues in his expression, his tone, his words. "Yeah, or whatever" could have real potential. Two times or maybe more? Maybe last night wasn't a mistake.

I snuggle back under the covers. A few moments later, my alarm goes off, startling me. Shit. I leap out of bed and rush to the shower. I almost forgot. I have my first class this morning teaching at NYU's business school. Newbie gets the Saturday morning class for full-time working professionals. I'm only part time on a probationary basis, but if it goes well, there's a possibility I could be brought on full time. My dad went to college with the dean of the business school, so that was my in. The dean also liked the fact that I have an MBA with several years' management consulting experience from a prestigious firm, where I helped companies navigate organizational change. In fact, that's exactly what my class is about —managing organizational change. It's an elective class in the leadership track. I'm hoping to teach more classes next semester on leadership as well as strategy. I'm pretty psyched about it, actually.

I turn on the shower, and while I'm waiting for it to warm up, I catch a glimpse of myself in the bathroom mirror. Wow, I look amazing! What a wonder orgasms can do for a woman. My skin is glowing and my usually limp blond hair has some body to it. Probably from rolling around on the mattress so much, but hey, I'll take it.

Focus! You can't be late for your first day of class.

I quickly strip and hop into the shower. I'll review my notes on the subway ride into the city. I really want this to work. This is the beginning of my new career. My parents are so proud that I'm taking up the profession they've dedicated their lives to. My dad teaches music at the local middle school, and my mom teaches first grade. I give myself a little mental pep talk to get pumped up. It's always an uphill battle to get past my natural shyness, but I won't let it stand in my way. *You're meant for this. It's in your DNA.*

The fact is, I love the material, and I love my new mission helping up and coming businessmen and women navigate the corporate world. Teaching is a higher calling, and I'm up for the challenge. I wash quickly and rinse off. *My three-hour class will be a total success. I work my life plan, and my life plan works for me. Go, go, go!*

A little over an hour later, I step out of the subway near campus, feeling groggy as I blink at the sun on a crisp fall day in late September. I need caffeine after staying up half the night. *Don't think about him. Focus, focus, focus.* I make my way to the corner coffee shop, staring out the window as I wait in line. I always loved September because I love school. *I'm meant for this. Today is the beginning of the best part of my life, fulfilling my destiny.*

The wait for coffee takes longer than I anticipated, and now I'm running late for class.

I speedwalk to the building, a little flustered and trying desperately not to be. *You've got this. You know your stuff. You're just going to share your stuff with other interested similarly minded people.* I've got on my lucky navy blue power suit, my new black pumps with a block heel, and I hope I'm still awash in orgasmic afterglow. *Don't think about that. It's a beauty miracle worker, though!*

The building is a beautiful, newer construction with a four-story rotunda, floor-to-ceiling windows, and lots of glass along the modern staircases. I dash upstairs to my second-floor classroom. It's one of the smaller rooms, not a huge auditorium.

Class starts in just a few minutes. I stop in the light-wood-paneled hallway just outside my very first classroom, a little winded, and take a few deep calming breaths before opening the door and striding confidently in. There's already a good crowd in here seated at long white tables in four tiered rows. Lots of white in here—the tables, the walls, and several white-boards at the front of the classroom. Three windows at the very back of the room add even more light reflecting off all the white.

I glance at my new students quickly, say good morning, and go straight to the front lectern. I should probably write my name on the whiteboard behind me, but I'm too jittery at the moment. I pull out my phone to keep an eye on the time, tuck my purse next to the lectern, and retrieve my notes and copies of the syllabus from my messenger bag. I plan to go over the syllabus, give a lecture, take a fifteen-minute break, and then have them discuss case studies in small groups. The class is on navigating organizational change in companies of all sizes, which is my specialty from my former management consulting career. I review my notes as a few more people arrive, check the time, and finally look up to start class. *Showtime.*

"Good morning, everyone. I'm Rebecca Edwards. Welcome to—" My breath whooshes from my body, my mouth gaping wide open, my stomach taking a horrible dive. This can't be.

I suck in air. What is he doing here? Hot Builder Guy, Connor *last name unknown like Prince,* is sitting in the back of my classroom, his piercing blue eyes locked on mine.

Oh God. What is happening right now? I can't seem to get a full breath. My heart is trying to escape my rib cage with its crazy pounding. Is this a heart attack?

I can't believe this.

Did he follow me here? Did I attract a stalker? No, wait. He was here first. He had to be. I would've noticed him walking in with his large size and muscles and sex appeal.

Crap! There's no way he could've known I'd be here. I never mentioned it. Which can only mean—

Hot Builder Guy is my student.

"Just a moment," I mumble through the roaring in my ears.

I stare at my notes, frozen in place for I don't know how long. Someone coughs, and I return to myself. I need to get things moving. These people didn't drag themselves to a classroom early on a Saturday just to watch their teacher stand catatonically in front of them. It occurs to me I have a class list. I'll take attendance and have people introduce themselves. Yes, an excellent idea. This will take the spotlight off me long enough to get my shit together. Also, I'll finally know whom I had multiple orgasms with last night.

Can I be fired for that?

My cheeks are fever hot. Actually, my entire body is hot and I'm a little shaky. I can't screw up my first job in my new career over some sordid teacher-student affair. I'm not going to be accused of anything inappropriate. No, sir, not me. I'll simply avoid eye contact and pretend he's not here.

"I'm going to take attendance," I announce, keeping my focus on my phone as I tap over to email to find the class list I received earlier from the registrar. "When I say your name, please share a little about your business background and what you hope to gain from this class."

I find the email and quickly scroll down the class list in search of a Connor. Not that I ever plan to see him again outside the classroom. Ah, found it. Crap. There's two Connors—Connor O'Sullivan and Connor Rourke. I don't even know which one he is! What am I supposed to call him, Connor O or Connor R? Because I know all I'll be thinking is Connor Orgasm Guy or Connor Renovation Guy or Connor Really Hot Sex Guy.

I am losing it.

Screw alphabetical order. I ignore the *A* last name sitting at the top of the list in favor of solving the Connor last name mystery. "Connor O'Sullivan." I keep my eyes on my phone.

A voice rings out from the front row. "That's me." I make

eye contact with a red-haired guy in his thirties and paste on a smile. He shifts in his seat to address the class. "I work at a start-up company and…"

I tune him out as I stare at the name I finally know. Connor Rourke. Something about that last name rings a bell. I stare at it blankly for long moments, my mind refusing to work. I need to do a Google search. Suddenly I realize the class is quiet. I quickly say another name, this time from the top of the list. "Michael Ahern."

Get real, you don't need to Google him. Obviously he's off-limits. And I know I'm kidding myself to expect someone as gorgeous and sexy and gruffly sweet as he is to wait three months for class to be over before dating me. Hell, he's probably a part-time MBA student, which means he'll keep taking classes for years, and I'll hopefully still be teaching here, which means Connor Rourke is forbidden.

My mind takes that moment to supply the missing information on his last name—the royal Rourkes. That's where I know the name. What if Connor is related to them? Does that make him a prince? Did I get naked with a prince? Is there any possibility at some point much later down the line when this class is over and we're both still conveniently single that I could visit the palace? Could there be a princess tiara in my future?

Ugh. I can't believe I'm off in la-la fantasy land. Prince or not, he's not an appropriate person for me to get involved with.

Hot Builder Guy, possibly a prince, is an MBA student. What are the chances? I'm so intrigued and dying to dive into Google to find out everything. Not that I'm going to do a thing about it.

"Anita Beecher," I announce during the silence.

Obviously, veering from the life plan was a huge error in judgment. Wait. Is that why he said he had no last name like Prince last night? Maybe he wasn't referring to the singer, but actually giving me a hint about his royal status. I rattle off a few more names for attendance, deep in thought, trying to remember what I heard about those royal Rourkes. Oh, yeah, there was a huge scandal when Princess Emma ran away from her own wedding to be with that gritty rock star Jackson Walker.

A few people laugh at something one of the students says, and I realize I'm not giving them my full attention. There will be plenty of time to satisfy my curiosity after class. The internet isn't going anywhere.

I go out of order to save Connor Rourke for last because I need to steel myself against his deep sexy voice.

"Yeah, I'm here, Rebecca Edwards."

My head jerks up at the sound of my full name. He's letting me know we both finally know the last name of the person we had wild animal sex with last night. Oh God. Can the other students tell I'm on fire with the memory and extremely embarrassed at the same time? Maybe I should pull the fire alarm. If ever a woman on fire needed a fast escape, it would be now. Except I would never break the rules by pulling the alarm in the case of no actual fire, and I'm rooted to the spot by the power of those intense blue eyes that seem to see right through me to my most vulnerable tender heart.

Connor goes on. "I work for my family's construction and real estate development business. Things have gotten more complicated since we took on real estate development, a lot to keep track of, and I came here to see what I could learn to help us navigate everything smoothly."

I tear my gaze away from him with no small amount of effort. "What an interesting and varied group." I grab my notes with shaking hands. "Let's get started. Most organizations, from start-ups to Fortune 500s, must change or fail." I have the entire lecture memorized, but I keep my eyes glued to it. I just need time to adjust to this unforeseen circumstance, just need to get through this first class.

Oh, shit. I forgot to go over the syllabus. I hand the stack of papers to the closest student. "Please pass these on."

I need to pull it together. Oh God, three months is a very long time.

∽

Connor

Three hours in the classroom for the first time in years and I can't focus. I'm having flashbacks to last night—

Becca at the bar looking so sexy with her lush red lips and long legs.

Those long legs wrapped around me.

Her throaty cries of ecstasy.

Her sweet enthusiasm.

My lover, my teacher. *Fuck me.*

I *knew* I shouldn't have signed up for this class. I never went to college and I had to get special permission to take it. I don't belong here, and I've been having doubts from the moment I registered. It's just that I'm stepping up in our family's company to second-in-command as COO (chief operating officer), my oldest brother Dylan's right-hand man. He's the CEO. I handle the day-to-day functions of the business while he plans and implements big-picture items. My brothers and I co-own Byrne Construction (originally my uncle's company on the Byrne side), along with the new company formed under it, Rourke Management, for real estate development.

I never thought I'd be the COO because my older brother Sean was always the one Dylan leaned on. It makes sense. Sean is the second oldest and tight with Dylan. But times are changing. Sean wanted to run our charitable branch—Royal Rourke Foundation US (the US branch of our cousins' foundation)—to bring in donations for stuff that adds to the community with each development we do, like parks and playgrounds. The real reason for his job change is because he fell hard for an actress, and he wanted the freedom to work on the go so he could follow her to different movie and TV locations. Actually, he texted just this morning that they got engaged last night when filming wrapped on her movie in Atlanta. So I guess that all worked out for him. As for me, I was the next logical choice to step into his role. Jack didn't want it, Brendan already has his niche seeking out new properties, and Beast is too young and inexperienced. I'm twenty-eight with ten years of work experience under my belt. Construction experience, not management experience.

I guess you could say this class was a kneejerk reaction to my own nerves about being COO. I started thinking maybe I don't know as much as I should to successfully manage our rapidly growing company. I just wanted to be as prepared as possible, especially knowing in a few months Dylan plans on taking paternity leave to be with his firstborn. Everything will be on my shoulders, and I can't let him down.

The moment class ends, Becca announces her office hours and quickly joins the line of students out the door without a backward glance toward me. I get the feeling she's avoiding me—she barely made eye contact the entire three hours—but we need to deal with this. I didn't miss how flustered she looked when she saw me sitting in the back of the room. I was just as shocked when she walked in. The wildcat from last night is a business school professor with an MBA and impressive job experience. I marvel for a moment that our paths crossed not once but twice. I don't think they normally would at all, but to happen twice? Maybe there's something to that.

I make it out to the hallway in time to catch her. She's talking to another student from class. I wait for the guy to leave and step close the moment she's alone. "Hey."

Bright red dots her cheeks. "Hi. Uh, I need to…" She gestures down the hall like she needs to go.

"I'll walk you out."

"This is inappropriate," she says under her breath, keeping to a fast pace.

"We're just walking. I didn't realize you were Rebecca Edwards."

"Becca is short for Rebecca," she mutters.

"And I didn't know your last name. This is all a bizarre coincidence."

She lowers her voice. "I knew last night was a mistake." She gestures wildly. "I always take my time, do my research—"

"Research?"

She gives me side-eye. "You don't Google people you get involved with?"

"Uh, no."

She lifts her chin. "Well, I do." She speeds up.

I keep pace with her. "Let's just look at the facts."

She shakes her head. "I should've reviewed the class list more closely."

"I never told you my last name. Remember how we joked about me being a one-name guy like Prince?"

The pink from her cheeks creeps down to her neck. She remembers the naked spooning when we had that conversation. If I hadn't been so tired, it would've led to forking right away. I suppress a smile at my own joke. I want to get back to that good warm feeling between us. I definitely don't want it to be over so soon.

"Becca, I know this is a shock for both of us, but it doesn't cancel out last night."

"Shh!" She stops walking and steps close to me. No red lipstick today. It's pink. A tempting pink. God, she's beautiful. "Obviously nothing further can happen between us. Please just delete my number and let's pretend last night never happened."

"What if I don't want to pretend it never happened?"

She narrows her pale blue eyes. "You have to. I'm only an adjunct professor, and this is my first class. I want this gig to work out."

I lower my voice to a husky tone. "What if I need extra help?"

She stiffens. "Then you can see me during my office hours on Thursday nights."

I cock my head. "Isn't that dangerous, you, me, an office alone at night?"

"I don't think you're taking this seriously enough," she says through her teeth.

I'm teasing, but clearly it's not the right time. "Trust me, I'm not gonna do anything that gets you in trouble." She nods once, and then the devil gets the best of me. "Unless you don't give me an A."

She gives my shoulder a poke. "This is not funny."

"It's absurdly coincidental. That makes it funny. Just a little."

Her mouth opens and then snaps shut. She turns on her heel and strides away, head held high.

I watch her go for a moment, trying to figure out what to do. We're going to see each other every Saturday morning. Possibly Thursday nights if I need extra help. *So wrong.* I swear I'm not usually so devilish. That's my brother Brendan. I'm the angel of my family. At least that's what my parents always used to say. I'm the fourth-born son, and they said I was such an angel they decided to have another. The next kid, Brendan, shocked them with his mischievous behavior. (They called him a "little devil.") I'm pretty sure Beast (Garrett) was an oops because after him my dad got snipped, and our family was set with five rambunctious boys and me, the angel. I'm not that angelic, just on the reserved side, keeping my thoughts to myself. Guess my parents appreciated a little quiet. Ha-ha.

I slowly walk out, keeping a distance behind her. I'm pretty sure we're heading for the same nearby subway stop. We both live in the Flatbush neighborhood of Brooklyn. I decide to stop for coffee to give her a head start. I'll catch a later train. Obviously she's not ready to deal with me as both her awesome lover and her so-so student. I smile to myself, remembering last night. She sure sang my praises then. I'll have to remind her of that next time I see her.

Outside the classroom of course.

5

I did it. I survived my first class, even with my unexpected student. I didn't pass out, flip out, or embarrass myself in any way. I head down the stairs to the subway. In fact, I'd go so far as to say today was a success. I even got myself an iced mocha coffee to celebrate. I take a last slurp from my drink and toss it in the garbage. Once I got past the first half hour, I relaxed, and I think we had some very thoughtful and interesting class discussion. Not from him. He was quiet. Thank God because I don't think I could've ignored him so easily if he was participating.

My shoulders slump as guilt creeps through me. It's really not fair to hope Connor won't participate for the rest of the semester. He signed up for this class to learn something, and that means being part of the group discussion. Next Saturday, during class break, I'll discreetly pull him aside and encourage him to participate. I'm sure, over time, it will get easier to hear his deep sexy voice and see his gorgeous *everything*. I exhale sharply. I'm being entirely shallow. My life plan says it's time for me to find a true partner, someone good for the long haul, someone *appropriate*. Connor Rourke is the exact opposite of what I need at this point in my life.

I'm pretty sure I can get fired for sleeping with a student. I don't dare ask anyone. I'll have to discreetly review the employee handbook. It's really dicey territory, especially for a brand-new adjunct professor on probation. I'm not sure I can hide the attraction if we keep seeing each other and I let myself get in deeper. What if the other students think I'm playing favorites? It would be so bad for my rep.

Firm boundaries are key.

I shift down the platform to wait for my train and pull out my phone. Just to close the Connor door completely, I look up the official policy on professor-student relationships. Yup, no surprise here. It's strictly prohibited, even at the graduate school level, and the only exception is extraordinary circumstances that have to be approved by your supervisor to eliminate any possible conflict of interest. There is no way I'm going to Dean Sears—my father's close friend from college— to ask special permission to continue to see the guy I hooked up with once. Me, a teacher on probation. I can't even imagine going there. Not only would it be excruciatingly embarrassing to ask my boss for permission, which he probably wouldn't grant, I'm sure Dean Sears would tell my dad. My parents would be so shocked and disappointed in me. They take their jobs as teachers very seriously— my dad was New York Teacher of the Year last year—and would never under any circumstance encourage a professor-student relationship. They'd never accept Connor. I'd be lucky if they didn't disown me.

Okay, so we had a good time and that is that. Eventually, I'll be able to comfortably teach class with him in it. All I need to do is keep those firm boundaries in place. Keep it professional.

I rock back on my heels. I really hoped last night was the beginning of something more. He's the first guy I ever hit it off with immediately. Everything felt so easy, so natural. I'm really bummed I can't follow up for more. Sometimes it sucks to do the right thing.

I refocus on my phone and tap over to Google. Privately doing research just to satisfy my curiosity about the royal thing is *not* crossing the line, I assure myself. On the walk over here, I remembered more about the Rourkes. When I was in England last spring for work, the royal Rourke wedding in nearby Villroy was on the news. It was a big deal that the groom was from the exiled family, and I'm pretty sure he was from New York. My heart kicks up at the thought that I might've been with a real prince last night. I type in "Rourke Villroy New York," and a boggling number of articles and images pop up. There's a lot about Dylan Rourke here.

I get the sudden sense that someone is staring at me, and lock eyes with the man himself. Not Dylan. The man who won't stop following me!

I quickly shove my phone back in my purse, my heart jackrabbiting, my cheeks flushed.

Connor tosses his coffee cup in the garbage before closing the distance between us. "Relax, I'm not following you. We live in the same neighborhood."

Oh, great, so we can take the subway together every Saturday, I think but don't say because I'm above such pettiness. *And I'll probably run into you around the neighborhood. Gah!* How am I supposed to keep firm boundaries when I keep seeing him everywhere? I'm only human and I'm incredibly attracted to him. Distance is my only defense against temptation.

"You don't have to look so appalled that we're neighbors," he says. "You seemed to like me okay last night."

I glance around, checking for any familiar faces from class. Coast is clear. Though I'm not sure I could pick out every one of my twenty new students in a crowd. I cross my arms and say in my sternest voice, "I shouldn't be seen with you outside of class unless it's during official office hours."

He studies me for so long I have to try not to fidget. *Does he suspect I was Googling him? Or that even now I'm finding it hard to resist him?* "You're really a stickler for the rules, huh?"

Oh, good, he doesn't suspect a thing.

I relax my arms. "In this case I am."

The screech of brakes announces our train has arrived. As soon as the doors clear of exiting passengers, I dart forward. I'm lucky enough to snag an empty three-person seat near the front of the car, which is the best kind of seat. See, it's not all awkward, excruciatingly embarrassing stuff today. I take the window seat and put my messenger bag in the center seat. Ah, space.

Connor drops down into the third seat, and I suppress a groan. Does he not get the urgency of this teacher-student-lover situation? We need distance.

A few moments pass and he just sits there quietly, like he's a casual stranger sitting on the subway when we both know he's more than that. I saw him naked. I kissed him, touched him, tasted him. I go damp at the lusty memory. *Getting off the porno brain train now. Not getting off, that also sounds lusty. Just halting it. Permanently. Porno brain train is now officially out of commission.*

I turn to him, determined to take control of the situation. "Do you not see the difficulty of the circumstances I find myself in? This is my first teaching job, and I really want it to go well. I'm only there on a part-time probationary basis. I can't screw that up in any way."

"You won't."

"I can't be with a student!"

He shifts to the middle seat, setting my messenger bag on his lap, and whispers in my ear, "Would it help that I'm auditing the class and not getting an official grade? I got special permission to take the class from one of the assistant deans."

I let out a small breath of relief that it wasn't the head dean he dealt with because that's my boss and my dad's good friend. Do *not* want that connection being made under any circumstances.

I shift to stare at him and we're suddenly very close, kissing close. I ignore the flash of heat that brings, ignore the thrumming of my pulse, and nonchalantly shift out of kissing range. "Why're you auditing?"

His voice is a silky caress—soothing, soft, drawing me in. "I'm not in the business school. I just wanted to learn more since I'm moving into a management position at work. I never went to college. I'd have to do that first before I could go to business school."

"Is this the only class you plan on taking?"

"Probably. It's not easy to fit in with work."

I lean back in my seat, thinking over this new info. One class, *my* class. I wouldn't have to avoid him for years. He's more like a visitor to the business school. Does that change things?

No, the optics are bad. He *looks* like my student. And there's no way he'd wait three months for me for class to end. We just met, and look at him, obviously he could have his pick of women.

Should I ask if he'd wait for class to be over to date me? But what if he sees this as a casual thing? Waiting for me would be more serious relationship territory.

"We good now?" he asks.

I sigh. "It's still a problem. It looks bad. I could get fired for being with a student."

"But I'm not getting a grade. Isn't that different?"

I still can't imagine asking Dean Sears for special permission to see Connor. How would I explain myself? We met at a bar the night before class, and I didn't know his last name, so the whole thing was a surprise. Even leaving out the hookup part, it sounds bad. Super casual and flighty. I need to look like the professor you want on staff full time. And I do not need this getting back to my parents.

"You still look like a student," I say firmly. "The other students will see you as one of them." *And I'll give myself away.* I'm not at all confident I can hide my attraction if I keep seeing him. The lusty memory bank will be full of many, many multiple orgasm nights. Ugh, this sucks. I finally found passion and now I have to kiss it goodbye. I don't even get that. Just a goodbye. No more wonderful kisses, no more wonderful orgasms from this wonderful man. Worst morning after ever.

He takes my hand, his thumb brushing the sensitive underside of my wrist. A hot shiver races up my arm. "I don't want you to get fired either, so what if we kept it quiet, ya know? Just between us."

I pull my hand away. I can't let myself be tempted. "No."

He faces forward. "Okay." He hands me my messenger bag.

I set it on my lap with my purse on top. *That's it, huh?* I thought he'd care a little more. He must've seen it as a casual thing between us.

I grind my teeth and turn away. Seriously, after all the dirty things we did to each other last night. I'm peeved and fully aware of the irony in that. I just can't help it. I hate to admit it, because I'm trying to stay strong and do the right thing, but it would've been nice if he was bummed too. I guess this is for the best. Sure, the sex would've been fantastic, but if it's not leading anywhere, then what's the point? That's not what I want. I know that about myself.

I glance over at him, and his eyes are closed like he's about to take a nap. *Seriously? He sits right next to me in a three-seater and ignores me?*

I whisper in his ear, "See, you just proved my point. You're not serious about us, so why would I risk my future just for sex?"

He doesn't bother to open his eyes. "What sex? I forgot about it, like you said."

I slump in my seat. I did tell him to forget it, but does he have to be so agreeable?

"That's fine," I assure him. "I forgot about it too."

He smiles, his teeth flashing white against the dark scruff of his jaw. "No, you didn't."

So cocky, so arrogant, so damn sexy. I refuse to be drawn in. The only course of action is to ignore him. We have to learn to coexist without interacting too closely if we're going to make it through the semester.

I pull my phone from my purse and tilt it away from him in case he opens his eyes. A few taps later, I'm scrolling through the Dylan Rourke wedding pictures. *Oh my God, it's him!* Hot Builder Guy really is a secret prince. Ooh, this is bad. He's a double fantasy for me, wrapped in one package—a royal renovator. What are the chances I'd meet a guy who ticks all my fantasy boxes? Before I got hooked on hot builder shows and that whole shirtless-guy-with-tools fantasy, I had my prince fantasy. He'd whisk me away to his palace, where I lived as a princess with all the beautiful clothes and horses a girl can dream up. (I was a bit younger when that fantasy started, but it's still exciting to think about.) How am I supposed to resist temptation for three long months? Especially knowing he's a multi-orgasm-giving royal renovator. So unfair.

I glance over at him still resting with his eyes closed. "You're a prince."

He opens his eyes a crack. "Are you Googling me?" He sounds amused.

"Why didn't you tell me you were a prince?"

He closes his eyes, a smug expression on his gorgeous face. "Too bad you're not interested, cuz I'm a catch."

"Whatever," I mutter.

Since his eyes are still closed, I immediately go back to Google and learn the fascinating, complicated history of his family's tie to this faraway kingdom. His father abdicated the throne to marry for love. So romantic! No wonder Prince Connor carried me when I fell. He's got those gallant royal manners in his genes.

I let out a small wistful sigh and suddenly realize the train stopped and Connor is standing. It's my stop. I grab my stuff and hurry out.

He follows me. *Ah, hell. Watch he lives down the block from me.* This is the universe's way of reminding me that veering from the life plan just makes a mess of things. That's why I have a plan in the first place.

"You can relax," he says as we climb the stairs to the street. "I'm three blocks away from where you live. You'll only see me if I want to see you."

I keep my eyes forward and work for a cool, even tone. "That's no problem. You live your life and I'll live mine. Just don't go back to The Twisted Chord." He's new to the neighborhood, and it's my go-to bar. I love it for the live music and the convenience to my apartment. He can find someplace else to pick up women. I sure don't want to witness it.

"Why, you calling dibs on the place?"

"Yes. I've been going there for years, and I never saw you there before last night. I've earned dibs."

We reach the sidewalk, and he keeps walking with me toward my building. "What if I want a beer?"

"Then you can buy a six-pack at your local liquor store."

"You mean the one on your block?"

"Wherever."

He grabs my arm, stopping me. His jaw is clenched, frustration clear in his voice. "Do ya want me to drop the class?"

My gut tightens and I swallow hard, swamped with guilt. "No, I don't want that. You have every right to be there. I hope you find it useful."

"Okay. So at some point you'll stop being hostile toward me?"

I'm taken aback. I was only trying to establish firm boundaries. "I'm not hostile. I was just thrown for a loop. I'll be fine by next week. Promise."

He inclines his head, and we keep walking in silence. My mind is a tangle of conflicting thoughts. I still want to see him, but I know how hypocritical and wrong that is. It's just that he's all these things I find fascinating—a prince and a builder—and by far the best lover I've ever had. I bet he's so skilled with his hands. He can probably do that intricate woodworking I love on crown moldings and antique furniture.

"Are you good at your job?" I finally ask.

"Yeah, I think so."

"What do you do exactly?"

"I can do it all. My uncle, the former owner of our company, had me rotate on different duties. Sheetrock, plumbing, electrical, roof—"

"Woodworking?"

His lips curve up, his blue eyes twinkling with good humor. "Yeah, I've been known to work some wood." He's flirting.

"I'm not touching that."

"Damn."

I bite my lower lip. This is just like my *Reno Magic* fantasy, where I'm at the work site with the gorgeous host, Clint Owens, and we're bantering about the tools and wood and stuff, and then suddenly we're going at it on the recently restored original hardwood flooring. *No. I must remain strong.*

A few moments later, we arrive at my building. His eyes search mine. "Looks like we're at your place." He wants to know where he stands. Maybe he senses my confusion. My brain and my body are in battle for supremacy of the right path. And my heart doesn't know what to do. I don't know where I stand with him. I don't know if it's worth risking my career over what we have, which is really just the one night.

"Con," I say because this is really between Con and Becca from last night, not student/royal renovator Connor Rourke and Professor Rebecca Edwards. And, the truth is, he's not just fantasy material, he's a real man with real feelings that I don't want to toy with. I know the right thing to do. I just have to find the strength to do it.

His voice is husky, making my knees weaken. "Yeah, Becca."

I open my mouth and shut it again. *Deep breath. Rip off the Band-Aid.* "See ya next week in class."

He backs up a step, his jaw tight, before giving me a terse nod and heading on his way.

I did the right thing. I'm sure of it. So why does my chest ache like I just lost something important?

6

———

Connor

I drop heavily into a folding chair at the makeshift lunch table, which is just a sheet of wood balanced across sawhorses, and grunt a hello to the guys—Brendan, Beast, and some new crew members. My sleep has gone to shit. It's been two days since my *accidentally hot for teacher* moment. I refuse to think about our night together, which is easy during the day when I'm busy enough to stay distracted. The problem is at night. I toss and turn before I finally fall asleep, and then I dream about her, waking up rock hard. Her soft skin, pale blue eyes, lush pink lips—all of her is burned into my brain. I need to forget her, I know that, but it's impossible. It's just that we seemed to click. We laughed at the same things, conversation was easy, and the sex was fantastic. What are the chances that I'd run into her twice in two days? I just moved to the neighborhood, so meeting her at the bar was one thing. Everyone is new to me there. But what are the odds I'd then see her at NYU?

Stop thinking about her!

I unwrap my usual lunch sandwich—potato chips on top of roast beef and provolone—and listen to the chatter around the table, something about an underground club. We staffed up for this project, which is why I don't know some of the crew that well. We're renovating an old marine rope factory in the former industrial waterfront area of Brooklyn into loft-style commercial space, hoping to attract tech and artsy design tenants. There's lots of light from the high arched windows, and the view of the Manhattan skyline is spectacular. Part of our philanthropic idea for this space is to include affordable art studios for people who need a large space to work with their materials, like woodworkers, metal workers, and ceramic artists. The surrounding land needs a rebuilt pier, which will eventually become part of a small waterfront park with a walking path and a grassy space for sunbathers and picnickers. It's our most ambitious project yet, and I'm feeling the pressure being in on the business side, especially since our family is financing it. Thankfully, continuing to work on crew as well helps keep me sane. I could never just be a desk job kind of guy.

Brendan picks up his phone and groans. "Who added Mom to our group text? Come on! My phone is blowing up with notifications. Not everything we say in the group is made for her eyes." The guys on crew snicker. My brothers and I have a group text.

He scrolls through the texts, muttering, "This is gonna bite us in the ass." He lifts his head, looking at me and then Beast. "Whoever did it, get her out."

"But she'll notice if we boot her," Beast says, giving himself away. "I just thought it would be easier to find a date that worked for everyone for Sean and Josie's engagement party."

Brendan shakes his phone in the air. "She won't stop texting."

"Make a separate group text without her," I say.

Beast starts tapping away at his phone. He's the baby of the family. Mom calls him her teddy bear. It's probably why he bulked up so much, just to get rid of that nickname. I'll admit he looks more like a beast than a teddy bear now. Especially since he got a buzz cut. The short hair really makes his face look more angular and tough. All smoke and mirrors to hide his secretly sensitive side.

My older brother, Jack, takes a seat and sets a bottle of hot sauce on the table. His dark brown hair is longish on top, styled with some product that makes him look more hipster than he is. He casually unwraps his sandwich. "Anyone want some hot sauce? It's a new blend from Lola." That's his friend's restaurant. As far as I know, they don't sell to-go condiments.

Nobody makes a move for the hot sauce. Jack is king of the pranksters, and we've all been burned before, even the new guys. Especially the new guys. Too bad for them because Jack is now crew chief.

"You have some first," I say, taking a bite of sandwich.

"I already did," he says smugly. "It's on my sandwich."

"Let's see you take some straight from the bottle," I say.

Jack tries to look offended, widening his eyes. "Come on, now. You know I've scaled back on the pranks. My fiancée has opened my eyes to being on the receiving end of one." He loves saying *my fiancée*. He's said it like a hundred times already and they've only been engaged three weeks.

Brendan laughs. "She did get you pretty good back in Vegas."

"Not the only time," Jack says.

Everyone erupts with questions about what else she did.

He holds up a palm. "I'm not sharing the grisly details. Just to say I've been schooled by the devious woman." A goofy smile spreads across his face as he opens a bottled water. He has no clue what a dope he looks like with all his dreamy smiles. Jack in love is both irritating and entertaining. It's his first time actually having a relationship, and he went all in. I'm happy for him, but I gotta give him a little trouble. It's what we do.

I snap a picture of his ridiculous expression and show it to him. "Look at the goof."

He grins. "That's what a man in love looks like." He grabs the hot sauce and shakes some right on his tongue. "See? Just hot-hot-hot." He grabs his water and chugs it, his face red.

Everyone cracks up.

"Bread will help better than water," Beast says over the laughter.

We all toss a piece of bread from our sandwiches at Jack's head. He laughs and then coughs like crazy.

"It's really not that hot," he claims on a gasping breath. "Just don't take it plain."

Dylan, our oldest brother and CEO, walks in, saying in a booming voice, "Hey, all! Looks like I'm just in time for lunch." He resembles my dad more than the rest of us, not just his features, but also his innate confidence and bearing. Dad and Dylan are both natural leaders. Only instead of being the king and the crown prince respectively, they became head of the family and CEO. They're still leaders in every important way.

"Why're you in such a good mood?" Brendan asks around a mouth full of chips. "Did you get a new lead on a property?"

Dylan told us he had an appointment this morning, but he didn't share what it was about. I'm not sure what Brendan's thinking. We don't have the funds to purchase another property while we're still working on the current one.

"Did the water tower clear?" I ask since that's our biggest headache right now.

Dylan's smile dims. "No to both. Con, we need to talk about the water tower." He crosses to us and holds up his phone. "It's a girl. We just did the ultrasound."

We all lean forward, squinting at a grainy black-and-white blob.

"How can you tell?" Brendan asks.

Dylan's jaw clenches.

"Congratulations," Beast says, and we all chime in with a belated congratulations.

"I still can't tell it's a girl," Brendan says, getting up and walking around to look over Dylan's shoulder. "What's that long thing?"

Dylan palms Brendan's face and shoves. "It's the umbilical cord, ya idiot. There's no penis. See? It's a girl." Dylan stares at his phone, a wide smile breaking out on his face. "A daughter." He takes us in, his eyes watering. "I'm gonna be a dad." He shakes his head, still seeming a little surprised by it. "Can you believe I'm gonna be a dad?"

I swallow over the lump in my throat. My older brothers are all settling down, getting married, getting engaged, and now Dylan is going to be a dad soon. And here I am stuck on a woman I can't have. My gut churns, my eyes gritty from lack of sleep. I hate that I feel jealous. It's just that Dylan looks so happy and I'm anything but. That's it. I'm going to see her again. I'm not sure where or when; I have to play it just right. We'll talk face-to-face and figure out a workaround where we can still be together.

I turn to Dylan. "You'll be a great dad. You always looked out for us when we were kids." I catch Jack's eye. "Remember when he punched Andy Wilson in the nose for stealing our lunches?"

"Yeah, that was awesome," Jack says. "Andy Wilson. What a wanker, stealing from younger kids."

Dylan slowly sinks to the empty chair next to me. "Oh, shit. I know what to do with brothers. I never had a sister. A girl is a whole different ball game."

"Ariana has a sister," I say. "She'll know what to do." That's his wife. She grew up next door to us, a quiet bookish girl. I kinda had a crush on her back in the day, but she was four years older, so there was no chance.

He scrubs a hand over his jaw. "Ariana is the younger sister. Rosalie looked out for her. I don't think she knows what to do either." He looks around the table, seeming to be searching for answers. None of us are dads. The new crew guys are always talking about parties and hookups. We all quietly go back to eating lunch, out of suggestions.

Brendan takes his seat across from me and lifts his chicken parm sub, holding it just shy of his mouth. "Don't worry about it, Dylan. I'm sure girls are just the same as boys." He takes a bite of sandwich, chews, and goes on. "Except for their hair." He swallows his food and continues in a thoughtful tone. "And ribbons and dresses and all that pink..." He trails off at Dylan's stony look and takes a big bite of his sandwich. I'm pretty sure there's more to raising a girl than hair and dressing them right, but damned if I know how to raise a girl either. They were a mystery when I was a kid and are only slightly less so now that I'm an adult. Their thought process is so complicated, and every nuance seems to matter. I don't think my tone or expression means half of what some of my exes claimed. I'm really what you see is what you get, no deep secret meaning hiding in what I say.

Dylan lets out a breath. "I'll figure it out. That's why I'm taking three months off in the beginning—to form that bond right off the bat."

My shoulders tense. That's the main reason I was made COO so quickly, so I can step into his shoes during his absence. I can't screw this up.

"Until the teen years," Jack puts in unhelpfully with a grin. He's always causing trouble. Thankfully he's got *a fiancée* now to rein him in. "Just don't let your daughter date some loser."

"Not helping," Dylan bites out.

"Ignore him," I say.

Dylan claps me on the shoulder. "Helps to know I've got Con here at the wheel while I'm on leave. Speaking of, I need you to go to a meeting in the city tomorrow about the water tower."

I stifle a groan. That tower is an eyesore on our property—rusted and covered in graffiti—but local residents see it as a historic landmark and want it to stay. It's right in the middle of our future park area and could be a hazard if kids decide to climb it. It's a lawsuit waiting to happen, if you ask me.

I turn to him. "I'll take care of it."

He nods once, looking pleased, and goes back to staring at his blurry baby picture. "I knew I could count on ya, Con."

～

The next day I drag myself down the sidewalk toward home. I'm running on fumes after an exhausting government meeting and terrible sleep because *she* haunts my dreams.

More meetings loom in my future, too, since this one ended with no final decision. Status: more deliberation needed. It's late enough in the day, around four, where going back to work doesn't make sense. I could use some caffeine. I'm not enjoying all these meetings. I'm used to being hands-on, getting shit done, taking action. None of this slow stakeholder talk, talk, talk. This is only our second real estate development project for Rourke Management. The first, converting an old elementary school into commercial office space with a wheelchair-accessible playground in back, was a huge success. We earned a commendation from the local town council for adding to the neighborhood's value, as well as awards for urban excellence and social responsibility. Those should be points in our favor, but there's some very vocal residents in this new project who believe we're trying to erase their history.

I stop at a coffee shop and get in line, thinking I should splurge for a double shot of espresso, even though I usually just get the regular house joe. I'm careful with my money since I'm saving to buy my own place. But I'm supposed to go into the city tonight to watch my soon-to-be sister-in-law Josie do standup comedy (my older brother Sean's fiancée, the actress/comedian). I don't want to sleep through it. Josie's a ball of infectious energy, so I imagine she's really funny at the mike. It'll be the first time I see her perform.

A dad holding a toddler on his shoulders shifts forward in line and I still, the hair on the back of my neck rising. It's *her*. The woman who haunts my dreams. Becca's a barista, expertly working the coffee machines. Adrenaline fires through my veins, and I'm suddenly more awake and alert than I've been since…the last time I saw her. This is the *third* time I've run into her completely randomly. I can't just ignore this. It's like I was meant to be part of her life. Why else would she keep showing up in my path? I don't usually stop for afternoon coffee in my neighborhood during the week. I'm usually at work. And why is she working here? I thought she was a professor.

I place my order with the cashier and shift to the end of

the long counter to wait for it. Becca hasn't noticed me, her eyes on her work. I watch her adding foam, mixing, and capping multiple cups. I can't help but think there's a reason I keep running into her. We can't ignore this thing between us just because of the strange circumstances we found ourselves in. I'd been thinking of asking her to meet for a drink somewhere, but Fate has other plans. I'm going with it.

She's busy so I keep quiet until she announces my name for my drink order and looks to see who Connor is. Does she hope it's me?

I smile. "Hi, Becca."

She squeaks and slaps a hand over her mouth, her eyes wide. I accidentally scared her.

"I didn't know you worked here." I lower my voice. "Why do you work here?"

She drops her hand from her mouth. "Stalker alert."

"I swear I'm not."

"Okay, stalker."

"I'd be hovering around your apartment building if I was any kind of decent stalker. Besides, aren't you the one who Googled me?"

Her expression softens as she gazes at me for a moment in what almost looks like wonder before saying, "I need to get back to work."

"When's your break?"

She goes back to filling drink orders. "I get off in half an hour. Why?"

"Could we talk then?"

She freezes in place and slowly turns to me. "About what?"

"Stuff." I can't say this shit in front of everyone here. "How're you doing?"

She sighs and returns to work. "Don't worry about me. I have a life plan."

I think fast, not willing to let go of this opportunity. "And I'm in need of a life plan. I'd like to hear what's involved from the expert."

She turns to me, a smile tugging at her lips. "Okay, fine.

I'll give you life plan pointers if you're willing to answer some questions that have come about by way of Google."

"Does it have to do with Villroy?"

She smiles big time, her eyes lighting up. "Yes."

I never play the prince card.

I'm totally going to play the prince card.

"Deal."

7

—————

Connor

A half hour later, Becca joins me at a small table near the front of the shop. "I only get fifteen minutes." She opens a bottled water and takes a long drink. "You want to explain why I keep running into you?"

I shrug one shoulder. "I was surprised to see you here. I usually don't stop by in the afternoon, but I got out of work early. I've only been here a couple of times on the weekend."

She jabs a finger at me. "Swear you're not a stalker?"

I hook my pinky finger with hers. "Swear on my sister's life."

"You don't have a sister."

I laugh because I caught her. She researched me, which is what she says she does before she goes out with someone. "I'd say of the two of us, you're more of a creeper, reading up on my family online."

She blushes and then whispers, "What's it like being royal?"

I lean across the table, whispering back, "I'm a secret royal, so it's like no one knows."

"And?"

"And since no one knows, they treat me exactly like I'm a

guy from Brooklyn." I lean back and lift a palm. "Whatta ya know, I *am* a guy from Brooklyn."

She sits back, frowning. "You said you would share details."

I'm doing a terrible job of playing the prince card. "Truth is, when you grow up hearing your dad was kicked out of his kingdom for marrying your mom and all of us were called riffraff, well, it doesn't give you warm and fuzzy feelings about royalty."

She props her head on her hand, a dreamy smile on her beautiful face. "What's the palace like?"

This is a woman with a prince fantasy. I have to indulge that for both our sakes.

I try to put some enthusiasm in my voice. "Okay, imagine what you think a royal palace would look like from a storybook or one of those animated princess movies. It's like that. A big stone monstrosity with turrets and spires."

She nods vigorously. "I saw a picture taken from afar online. It's so beautiful. Is there a moat?"

"No, just a large courtyard in front."

"What's the inside like?"

"Like a museum."

She waves me on. "Come on, details!"

I think back to when I visited last spring for Dylan's wedding. I was there for my cousin Adrian's wedding too. "Two-story white marble entrance hall with silk wallpaper and a crystal chandelier. An enormous ballroom with inlaid wooden floors, gold wallpaper, ceiling frescoes, even more chandeliers. Way too many rooms. It's like a maze trying to find your way around. East wing and west wing form a courtyard in back with formal gardens made of sculpted hedgerows and geometric plantings."

She sighs. "Wow. You're so lucky. I saw pictures of you and your brothers at Dylan's wedding there."

"Yup. That's me. Prince Connor Rourke at your service." *Look at me getting the hang of the prince fantasy.*

She smiles, looking up at me under her lashes. "I can't believe I know a real prince."

"So you're really into the royal thing, huh?"

She leans back, her cheeks and neck flushed pink. "It's interesting." She guzzles her water. She definitely is. It almost makes me want to get in touch with my cousin Adrian about a visit just so Becca can see the palace, but one thing at a time. My cousin is real accommodating like that, and it's even easier to travel there because of the royal jet. First, I need to get Becca comfortable enough to agree to see me again.

"Your turn," I say. "Tell me more about this life plan stuff."

She purses her pink lips. My mind immediately goes to a dirty place. *Must. Stop. Dirty. Thoughts.* "Do you really want to know, or are you going to make fun of me?"

"I really want to know."

She sets her water down. "Basically, you do an inventory of your life and where you'd like to see yourself in various categories—work, health, personal—and then you work backwards, breaking down the steps to get there. I took a one-year, three-year, and five-year view, but you can vary that according to your needs."

"So it's like a business plan for your life."

"Exactly!"

"See, I already learned something from your class."

She deflates, looking away. "Uh-huh, good."

Idiot. Why did I have to bring up class? It's the whole reason she's worried about getting involved with me.

"I'd like a life plan," I say. "Tell me about yours so I can reverse engineer one of my own."

She eyes me suspiciously.

I lean forward. "I'm serious. I want to know." *Mostly so I can get to know you better.* Seeing Becca today makes all the restless nights worth it. Just hearing her talk and seeing her smile makes my shoulders relax.

"Okay. On the work side, I decided I wanted to go into teaching. It's something my parents do and love, and I like the idea of helping people grow in their careers. So I got lucky and found something right away. Only adjunct for now, but it's a start. And teaching gives me a better work-life balance.

Before I was working hundred-hour weeks traveling all over the globe for work. I burned out. If I tried to keep going at that pace, I'm sure I would've started having serious health issues. I barely slept."

"And now you can sleep."

"Yes. I'm feeling more like my old self again."

"How many jobs do you have?"

"Just two. I work here part time for the health insurance benefits. My boss wants to make me manager, but I'm trying to give myself some breathing room."

She must've been bringing in bank at her old job if she can only work part time and keep her nice apartment. That means she's a saver, like me. I file that one away.

She goes on. "For my health goals, I eat healthy, make sleep a priority, and I do some kind of exercise every day."

"So that's work and health." I lean in, my voice husky. "What's the personal?"

She ducks her head, rubbing the back of her neck. "What time is it?"

I check my phone. "You've still got seven minutes. We're fast talkers. You especially." Most New Yorkers talk fast.

She lets out a breath. "I'm working on taking it easy for one thing. Trying to be a little more laid-back."

Working at taking it easy sounds impossible, but I keep that to myself. "What else is in the personal goal section?" I'm pushing because I have a feeling it has to do with getting a guy. *And guess who's conveniently sitting across from you? The guy you had mind-blowing sex with last Friday night.* I definitely blew her mind. She couldn't stop praising me. *Wonderful man.* No one's ever called me that before, especially with her enthusiasm. I hear it in my dreams.

She takes a drink of water, eyeing me over the bottle as she stalls for time.

I wait her out because I suspect, deep down, she wants to share.

She sets her water down, her voice so soft I have to lean in. "I'm twenty-nine and I want to be settled into a mean-ingful relationship by thirty, so I accept one date per week every Friday for drinks. I have one this Friday actually, right on schedule. That's what it means to have a life plan, you work the plan and the plan works for you."

I straighten. She has a date this Friday? I drag a hand through my hair, trying to figure out how to stop it or put myself in his place as the better option. Of course I'm the better option. We had a great night together. And there's no way he's a prince. *Come on! This can't just be one sided.*

Sweat trickles down my chest. I play it cool. "How do you make sure your personal goal happens according to plan every Friday for drinks? Isn't it kind of random who you meet?" *Like we keep meeting?*

She smiles. "That's the beauty of a plan, you see? I just follow the steps. First I do my research and—"

"Research for a relationship?"

She slowly shakes her head, giving me a sympathetic look. "You can't expect to find someone for a serious relationship at a bar pickup scene. They need to be vetted first."

I can't help but ask. "By Google?"

She laughs. "That comes later. Anyway, I accept one date per week, and if we don't click within the first hour, then I move on."

My chest puffs out. I made it well past the first hour. It occurs to me that she meets her dates at The Twisted Chord for drinks, which is why she was there alone last Friday, except last week's guy stood her up. That's probably also why she doesn't want me to go there. She's got a plan—Friday night date for drinks at the bar closest to her place. *For a convenient sexual-compatibility check afterwards?* No. She said she never does that when she first asked me over. Plus, she seemed nervous in the beginning and embarrassed after. I was the exception. Definitely something special here.

And that means she's on a search for a serious relationship guy. I wouldn't say I'm looking to settle down, but I'm not anti-relationship either. My parents have a good marriage and my family is close. My older brothers—Dylan, Sean, Jack —all found women they're crazy about. Maybe it's my turn. Why else would I keep running into her? It would also explain why I can't stop thinking about her, dreaming about her. I've never been so stuck on a woman before. I can't let her go on this date on Friday. What if she clicks with that guy?

Dammit, she clicked with me first and I don't want her to move on. *Keep cool, think it through.*

"Where do you find the dates?" I ask.

She lowers her voice. "I did my research and found the best online dating service for people seeking serious relationships."

See, I was right? She's on a quest. For me.

"You mean New York Edge?" I totally made that up.

"No, eLoveMatch."

Bingo!

Her brows furrow. "I've never heard of New York Edge."

"I dunno. I thought I heard Beast mention it before. Supposed to give you an edge on dating, like you're already matched so well it's like date two instead of date one."

"Really?" She picks up her phone to look it up. "Maybe I'll try it."

I put my hand over her phone. "It's not for serious relationships."

"But you said they're well matched."

"Yeah, so they can feel comfortable moving forward with the hookup faster. Hookup with potential, no heavy expectations." *Kinda like us last Friday night.*

"Oh." Her lips part as she holds my gaze. She's remembering our night. This is good.

She gestures vaguely behind her. "I'd better go. Bathroom break and then back to work." She stands and offers me her hand. "Good luck with your life plan."

I cross to her and give her hand a squeeze. "You too, Becca. See ya around."

She shakes her head, smiling. "Yeah. Just not too much, creeper."

I grin. "You'd better delete my picture from your screensaver." I'm sure she saw me cleaned up nice in a tux for Dylan's wedding during her online research on me.

Pink dots her cheeks. "I don't have your picture as my screensaver! Arrogant much?"

"Keep it on your phone, though." I wink. "Your secret prince."

She tucks her hair behind her ear. "Ridiculous. You're not...I don't even..." She meets my eyes, guilt written all over her face. She did save my picture from the internet. "I'm going now."

"Bye, Becca."

I turn and walk out the door. There's definitely something here, and now I've got a plan that places us squarely on the same path. It's a go.

As long as we're not caught.

∾

Becca

It's Thursday night and I'm sitting in a small office at the university for my class office hours. It's quiet at this end of the hall, only a few night classes going on in the building. I left the door open, and every little noise makes my pulse pick up. I can't help but wonder if Connor is going to show up. He did show up at my other job completely randomly. If he shows up here, it will mean something significant. Because now he knows exactly where I stand on wanting a relationship. If he still wants to pursue me, I'm not sure what I'll do. Do I dare risk my career for a chance at the kind of relationship I've been longing for?

There's no question in my mind what would happen if anyone knew—fired with a black mark against me, never to work in academia again. That kind of violation of the rules follows you around. And those rules are in place for good reason. I'm just not sure my situation is the kind administrators thought of when they put it in place. After all, it's completely consensual. If anything, Connor is the one pursuing me, not the other way around. And we met before I knew he was my student. Yes, I'm rationalizing.

He could show up. I practically invited him, saying this

was the appropriate place to talk to me. I fan myself with the syllabus, Connor's husky voice sounding in my mind. *What if I need extra help?*

And me: *Then you can see me during my office hours on Thursday nights.*

Hot Builder Guy/Secret Prince/Best Lover I've Ever Had: *Isn't that dangerous, you, me, an office alone at night?*

I set the syllabus down and smooth my hair. I hope he doesn't show up because that would be inappropriate, and I can't let myself get carried away. I mean, if he walked in here right now with his charming smile and deep sexy voice and kissed me—

My mind flashes to that night. Connor pinning me against the wall, his mouth demanding on mine. His big calloused builder hands, his hard body, his intoxicating scent. All those wonderful orgasms he gave me. My skin flushes, a low ache in my belly reminding me of how greedy I was, still am, for more. One kiss would be all it took. Next thing you know, we'd be going at it on this sleek metal desk—hot skin against cool metal, stop! Someone would see us and I'd be fired. Losing my job, the shame of facing my parents, ending my newfound career so soon—I just can't go there.

I close my eyes and take a deep breath. If he shows up, I'll tell him we'll talk while we take a walk down the hallway. I congratulate myself on this clever plan. We'll be out in public, so no chance of something intimate, and I'll still be able to see if another student shows up at my office.

I check the time on my phone. I'm fifteen minutes into my hour. They call it office hours, but it's actually only an hour. Some professors offer them multiple times a week, but I was only required to have the one. Hmm, I wonder if anyone will show up. The dean encouraged us to have an open-door policy and assure our students that they can stop by just to talk. They don't even need to have a question. It's all about us professors getting to know our students and their aspirations so we can be a source of support in their career goals. They're very student-centric here. Though, to be honest, it was similar at my business school, and I think I went to office hours maybe twice in the two years I was there.

I jump at a knock on my door, my heart racing. "Hello, come in." I smile at the man who is not Connor Rourke, trying to hide my disappointment. Why can't I stop thinking about him? I know he's off-limits.

"Mike Ahern," he says, striding in and offering me his hand. I reach out, and he gives me a firm handshake before taking the seat across from me. He's probably in his thirties with short blond hair in a side part. In class, it was obvious he was a go-getter, talking loud and fast, dominating the discussion.

"Yes, I remember your name. How do you like class so far?"

"Excellent. Great start and I'm really glad I signed up for it. The case study on coffee was fascinating. I never thought about the difference between fair trade and direct trade. You hear about fair trade coffee all the time, and there's a premium for it, right, ha-ha, but which is better for the workers? What is the real end goal, and how do we ensure quality standards in the coffee?"

I barely get out a reply before he goes off on a long tirade over marketing practices and how some companies have co-opted the jargon without actually following through. He's quite passionate and it makes me think he's the kind of original thinker who'll one day do something important in the world.

When he finally winds down, I say, "Remind me what you do for work, Mike."

"I'm an IT project manager. Very important. People want their tech fully operational at all times and fast. Back to coffee. The supply chain fascinates me. I never really thought about that either." He launches into a lecture *very* similar to what I gave in class.

I open my mouth to talk a few times, but it seems there's no need. Mike is here to share with me everything I already shared, with a few repeat loops and his personal opinion. I almost feel like I'm the student and he's the professor, except he's literally parroting back what I've already taught. Maybe he's not such an original thinker after all. Geez, I really don't want to be stuck in another office hour with him. I'll be sure to remind my students on Saturday that I would very much like to see them during office hours to discuss each of their future goals and connect them with resources in any way I can. I only pray at least one more person shows up. What if I get a Mike lecture every Thursday night parroting back my lecture? *Kill me now.*

Finally, mercifully, the hour is up and I stand, gathering my light jacket and purse. "Well, Mike, it's time for me to go." I stuff the syllabus into my messenger bag. "I'll see you in class on Saturday."

He stands. "Wow. That hour went so fast."

I move around the desk and wait for him to head out. I'm supposed to lock the door when I leave.

He flashes a smile. "Hey, why don't we go for coffee and continue this conversation. Wouldn't that be great, drinking coffee while discussing it?"

"Actually, it's late and I really do need to go. Thanks, though."

"Sure, sure, no problem." He turns and walks out the door.

I follow him out and lock it behind me.

He offers his hand again and gives me another firm handshake. "Great talk. Look forward to the next class."

I have to give him points for enthusiasm. I smile. "Glad you're enjoying class."

He gives me a small salute with a too-bright smile before striding down the hall.

I let out a breath and head in the opposite direction. I don't think I've ever endured a more exhausting hour of conversation. And to think my biggest concern was Connor showing up.

My shoulders droop. Connor didn't show. I guess he's not pursuing me after all. I shouldn't have cancelled my Friday night date from eLoveMatch. I square my shoulders and pick up the pace. It's fine. I was clear about my future goals to him, obviously he's not on the same page, and the two of us together is too complicated anyway. Now I don't have to worry. Just life per usual, back to eLoveMatch for my next first date. There's always more potentially great guys in the app. I ignore the dread already building at the thought. I made a life plan for a reason, and I'm going to follow it no matter what.

8

Becca

So much for the stellar reputation of eLoveMatch. I can't believe this! Here I am, waiting at The Twisted Chord to meet up with yet another guy who can't be bothered to show up. I responded to Matt's invitation just last night after my excruciating office hour. He seemed delighted when I replied. You know, I'm going to email a very sternly worded letter to eLoveMatch and demand a refund. I check my phone. Still no messages and he's fifteen minutes late. I don't even care if he has some great excuse. I'm not going to sit here and pretend he got run over by a car. If he can't be punctual, he's out. I don't appreciate wasting my time. My eyes sting, and I swallow hard. Why is it so hard to meet someone new? Am I giving off an unapproachable vibe? It's not like I can smile the whole time I'm sitting here. Can I help it if I have resting bitch face?

I toss back my wine and decide it's a popcorn-for-dinner night curled up on my sofa, watching my favorite hot builder renovation show. Clint Owens from *Reno Magic* will be my date tonight. I pull some cash from my purse to pay for my drink just as a guy in a white shirt takes the seat next to me.

"Hey, Becca," a familiar sexy voice says.

I jerk my head up, my heart hammering against my rib cage. "Connor."

He smiles, and I find myself smiling back. He has such a warm smile that reaches his deep blue eyes, making tiny crinkles around them. He's dressed nice in a white button-down shirt with jeans and black boots. Casually hot.

"Hope you don't mind I'm back at our neighborhood bar," he says.

I forgot I told him to keep away. "Hey, it's Friday night. Enjoy. I'm heading out."

"Were you waiting for someone?"

I press my lips tightly together. I can't admit that my life plan is so screwed up after I just sang the praises of having a life plan and eLoveMatch in particular. I'm upset and getting a little paranoid about being stood up two weeks in a row. I turn his question around. "Are you here alone?"

One corner of his mouth lifts. "I was hoping to pick up someone."

I huff. *He acts like our night together meant nothing! Like I wouldn't care if he picked up someone in front of me. In my bar! I claimed the place!*

"Have fun," I say stiffly. I stand, turning to get past him when he snags my wrist.

His eyes are intent on mine. "I was hoping to pick you up. I'm the guy you're waiting for. Sorry I was a little late because of work."

My brows scrunch together in confusion. "No, I'm waiting for Matt Williams. He's a financial planner. Short dark brown hair, brown eyes, enjoys…" I trail off at his intense look and gulp. "You're serious."

"Matt is my friend's husband. I just used some of his details."

He's still holding my wrist and I like it way too much. I just stand there, staring at him while my mind whirls from shock to confused to—I hate to admit it—extremely flattered. He wants to see me again after knowing I'm looking for a relationship, and he made a real effort. On the other hand, he broke the rules and that does not bode well for professional rules, which absolutely can't be broken. What he did was completely unethical. Why am I so drawn to him? I wish I weren't. It's just too complicated.

"Con, you used his picture too. It's against the rules to impersonate someone else. I could have you banned from eLoveMatch for life."

"Okay."

He loosens his grip on my wrist and takes my hand in his, enveloping mine with warmth. He shifts, bringing us closer. I'm standing between his legs, and we're eye to eye. I don't know what to do. I didn't expect to see him tonight, and I convinced myself he wasn't into a relationship. Now he maybe is into it, but it's extremely risky. My parents would never accept me dating a student, never accept him. The levels of subterfuge I'd have to go through to make this work are way out of my comfort zone. And, yes, I'm working on getting out of my comfort zone, but lying is a step too far. Plus, I psyched myself up for a first date with Matt and all the work that goes into trying to present my best self while also looking for signs of potential in my date.

I'm so confused.

"You wanna stay for a drink?" he asks.

I look toward the bar, but it doesn't appeal. I know what I really want, and I think he'll understand. He did say he wasn't so into the bar scene anymore. "Honestly, I just want to go home, eat popcorn for dinner, and watch the Home Improvement channel."

"Perfect. I'll go with you."

For some reason I hadn't anticipated that. "You're just inviting yourself over?"

He holds me by the chin, his blue eyes twinkling with good humor. "Your secret prince loves the Home Improvement channel."

I can feel myself caving. He's touching me, he smells so good, and he loves to do what I love to do—watch hot builders at work. No, wait.

"Why do you love the Home Improvement channel?" I ask.

"What's not to love? Watching a project come together. It's always improved at the end. Plus I can secretly laugh when I know they way underpriced how much it would cost to do something. It's like they leave out the cost of labor."

It occurs to me he could really add a unique perspective, which could be fascinating. "Okay, but you shouldn't assume—"

"I assume nothing." He guides me forward and then walks me out, one hand on my lower back. The heat of his hand electrifies me, sparks radiating from the spot. Then he ruins it. "Now let me be up front with you, Ms. Edwards, I don't want to write that paper. That's not for me." He's addressing me as his teacher.

This is so wrong.

Still, my brain zeroes in on why he thinks writing the paper isn't for him. I think he lacks confidence in his academic abilities because he skipped college. I can tell he's smart though.

"Why don't you want to write it?" I ask and gasp in surprise as he lifts me through the front doorway, his arm anchored around my waist. And then my cheeks heat as I realize it's probably because of when I fell through this very same doorway.

He sets me down on the sidewalk and takes my hand, heading toward my place. "My grammar is atrocious."

I focus on his problem instead of my embarrassment. Besides, I kinda like the way he casually lifts me. "Do it anyway. It's part of class."

"You'll judge me."

"I'll judge you for not doing the work. Why did you sign up for this class if you weren't going to do the work?"

"To listen and see if I was missing out on any big business secrets."

"Are you?"

"I wouldn't say secrets, but it's interesting to hear how other companies tackle difficult problems. My view has been really narrow, working with the same crew for years on the same kinds of projects. Until recently. I can see how your class could be really helpful going forward. Especially with so much riding on our current project. There's a lot of money on the line and a lot of responsibility on my shoulders."

I try to hide my disappointment. I'm a terrible person because I was going to suggest, if he wasn't learning anything, he should just drop the class so we could get back to the fun stuff. *Bad teacher, very bad.* I can't ask him to quit the class for selfish reasons.

"I'm glad you find it useful," I say, attempting a smile.

"I really don't want to write the paper though," he says, pushing his advantage just because we saw each other naked.

I keep my voice firm. "There's a point to the homework, and that's to help you learn it on a deeper level. Writing the paper will ensure you put more thought into things on your own instead of just echoing back what I say in class." I think of how Mike did that during my office hours last night, but keep it to myself. I don't think I should bitch about another student to my current student. *Oh God. What am I doing?*

"Fine, Teach. I'll write the damn paper."

This is getting too deep into student-teacher territory, and I'm reminded of all the reasons I set a boundary between us.

I halt and pull my hand from his grip. "I don't think this is a good idea. You go watch TV at your place and I'll watch it at mine. You can text me your opinions on the renovation, okay?"

He stares at me with those intense blue eyes. I swear he can see right through me—all my conflicting emotions and my intense attraction to him. "Becca, here's the facts. We have insane chemistry—"

"Con—"

"Don't deny it. I can't ignore it. We both like renovation stuff, and I think we can have a good time together hanging out or whatever. Neither of us loves the bar scene anymore. Be honest, you're forcing yourself to show up for drinks every Friday night to meet someone, and you're not enjoying it. Well, you're in luck. You met someone, me, so you don't have to force yourself to do that."

"But—"

"I can't stop thinking about you," he says gruffly.

Oh, that's nice. Really nice. "Me too, but—"

"Bec." He strokes my hair back over my ear. "I told myself to leave you alone, but I keep running into you, and maybe that means something."

My pulse picks up, and something bubbles up inside me that feels dangerously like hope. He's warm, he's sincere, it's not just the physical for him. "It's risky," I whisper as if my boss were just around the corner. "For me. There's a lot on the line."

"I know and I swear I won't do anything to hurt your career." He takes my hand and gives it a reassuring squeeze. "No one has to know."

"Hiding a relationship from everyone—all the lies and deceit—I'm not sure I can do it. My boss, Dean Sears, is close with my dad, and my parents—both teachers, if you remember—would probably disown me over the scandal. Plus I'd be fired, never to work in academia again, and my entire life plan would implode."

He blows out a long breath, his brows drawing down. "Okay, I get it. Believe me, I wish the circumstances were different, but this is what we got. And I don't want to walk away from you, from us."

I want to deny him, but what comes out is simply his name said with all the longing I truly feel inside. "Con."

"Let's go."

I sputter as he practically drags me down the sidewalk. "There's still a major problem."

He stops and hauls me against him. "Kiss me."

I stare at him, my breath stalling, my mind going utterly blank. The heat of his body radiates through me, all of my softness pressed against his hard muscular frame. I'm so caught up in him.

He cups my jaw, his thumb stroking the sensitive spot behind my ear. "Please."

I comply because he said please, and it's just as wonderful as before. Sparks fire over my skin, the heat igniting between us. I wrap my arms around his neck and lose myself in the kind of passion I've only imagined before.

A long moment later, he breaks the kiss, his fingers trailing down the side of my neck, giving me a hot shiver. "Bec, other people have a problem, but there's no problem with *us*."

He backs away, and I desperately want him close again. Would anyone really know if he went home with me in Brooklyn? It's not likely I'd run into my NYU students here. They're probably hanging out in the city. But I'll still have to face him in class tomorrow morning. It would be impossible to hide the attraction. One look from his knowing bedroom eyes and I'd blush.

Why is it so hard to do the right thing?

"Con?"

"Yeah?"

"How about we pick up again after class ends? Then there's no issue."

He exhales sharply. "That's December. It's September now."

"Yes, but then it wouldn't be such an ethical quandary, and by then I'd know if they want to keep me on as a professor. There's a possibility I could be brought on full time."

He looks to the sky before leveling me with a hard look. "So you expect me to wait four months for you to decide if you want to watch TV with me on a Friday night?"

"Closer to three months. And you know it wouldn't just be TV."

He closes the distance and strokes my hair back over my ear before cradling my jaw with one large hand. "And how do I know that?"

My cheeks flush. "The insane chemistry. Something would happen. It's playing with fire."

"And you don't want to get burned."

"Exactly," I say softly.

"What if you just get toasty?"

I laugh.

His palm slides down my arm in a warm caress before taking my hand. "I'm not waiting around for four months.

That's just wasting time. Besides, what if you meet someone through that dating app, or I meet some other sexy professor?"

I narrow my eyes. "Why didn't you say a sexy grad student?"

He squeezes my hand and winks. "Guess I have a thing for teacher. Offer expires in ten seconds."

I pull my hand from his. "I don't appreciate the time pressure. You know I'm conflicted."

"I'm trying to get you to stop thinking so much and just feel. Us together feels good."

"It's more complicated than that."

"In or out, Becca? Last chance."

I park a hand on my hip. "I'll see you in class tomorrow." I turn on my heel and walk toward home. Geez. I don't appreciate the bossy demanding attitude. *Ten seconds. Hmph.* Just because I'm on the quiet side doesn't mean I don't have a backbone.

"If I see you at The Twisted Chord with another guy, I'm gonna have to say hi," he announces.

I whirl. "Is that some kind of threat?"

He shrugs. "Don't meet your guys in my neighborhood bar is all I'm saying. It's rude to the guy who offered to watch TV with you."

I march back to him. "That's *my* neighborhood bar. I already claimed it."

"You've been warned," he says like it's out of his hands.

I bristle. "What is your problem?"

"I don't have a problem."

"Yes, you do. A big one."

His blue eyes gleam, a small smirk on his face. "And that is?"

I throw my hands up. "You're bossy, you think you know everything, and you don't care about professional boundaries. Or personal ones!"

He cocks his head. "Now, Becca, if I knew everything, why would I be taking your class?"

I'm suddenly overheated despite the cool night. I peel off

my white cardigan and tie it around my shoulders. "And you're too calm about everything."

His lips curl up. "Too cool for school."

"Stop making school and teacher jokes!"

He snags my wrist in a loose grip, his thumb stroking the sensitive underside. I ignore the tingling heat radiating from the spot. "Sometimes I forget women can't take a joke."

"I can take a joke!"

"Then why're you getting so worked up?"

My cheeks are hot, actually all of me is hot. I'm agitated beyond belief, yet I can't seem to pull my wrist from his grip. It feels too good when he touches me. I stare at my traitorous wrist and watch as he turns it, exposing my rapidly beating pulse. His gaze collides with mine as he lifts my wrist to his lips and kisses the pulse point. I nearly swoon.

He lowers my hand, his fingers clasped firmly around my wrist so I can't make an escape. It's almost a relief to have him take control, keeping me close. "Bec." His voice is husky.

"Yes?" I breathe.

He leans close to my ear. "You know those renovation shows are fake, right? If I were there, I could tell you the real deal, which would be helpful if you're in the market for a home. Personally, I've been saving for years to buy my own place."

This is the sexiest dirty talk I've ever heard. "You're a saver?" So many men don't have that long-term planning ability. It's one of the things I look for in a guy, being a planner myself.

He smiles, and I feel myself weakening. "I'm a saver. I've eaten the same packed lunch for years to save my pennies."

My voice sounds throaty even to my own ears. I'm just so turned on. "Saving is actually a good quality. It says you can hold off on instant gratification and think long term."

He kisses my neck, working his way up to my ear. My knees weaken. "Is that what you look for in a guy?"

"Yes," I admit.

He meets my eyes, his breath fanning over my lips. "What else?"

I lean against him and realize it's because his arm is now banded around my waist. "I look for good health because that says he takes care of himself, a good relationship with his parents, and no heavy relationship baggage."

"Check, check, and check."

I'm melting. He's a saver, he's checking boxes, and he's holding me so close I can barely think. Still, I can't risk this if there's no reward. "Are you really looking for a relationship?" I ask softly.

He cradles my jaw, his gaze tender. "I wasn't looking, but somehow it found me."

I let out a swoony sigh. "Oh, Con."

His lips meet mine in a soft kiss. I throw my arms around his neck and kiss him back passionately.

Applause breaks out nearby. I break the kiss and turn toward the curious looks of a small group of twentysomethings hanging out by the bodega on the corner.

I catch Connor's eye, and we laugh. Guess we did put on a show. I grab his hand and head toward home. "Come on. We need privacy."

He laughs. "You don't need to pull my hand. I'll go of my own accord."

I pull harder. "Let's go, mister—ah!" He flipped me over his shoulder! More applause rings out.

Some guy calls out, "Show her who's boss."

I'm about to call BS on whoever said that when Connor casually replies, "She's got me good. Shh, don't tell her."

I beam and give his back a little squeeze. He gives my ass a squeeze back. This is all so inappropriate, yet I'm loving every second. "Why can't I resist you?"

"Easy. Because I'm irresistible."

I laugh. "Con, my head's starting to throb. Can you put me down?"

He shifts me so I'm cradled in his arms. "Better?"

I burrow my face against his chest. "People are staring."

"If I put you down, the blood's gonna rush from your head. You'll be dizzy and staggering around like a drunk. This is better."

I smile up at him. "When you put it that way."

"Plus this way I know you're not going to run off without me."

"We shouldn't be doing this."

"We shouldn't *not* be doing this."

I rest my cheek against his chest, his solid heat relaxing me. "That makes no sense."

"Double negative. Two wrongs make a right."

"But I'm always careful to be in the right with no wrongs at all."

"With me you *are* in the right. It's simple math. Con plus Becca equals…"

I lift my head to meet his eyes. "Equals what?"

He smiles warmly. "Something good."

I sigh happily and settle against his chest. There's something so nice about being tucked close against him. Like nothing can touch me in the safety of his arms.

He sets me down a few minutes later by the front entrance of my building. I let us in and we head to the elevator. My mind flashes back to last Friday when we were in this elevator—my nerves, the crackling tension in the air, that kiss. Only this time, Connor stands with his hands at his sides, looking straight ahead. He seems kind of serious now.

We get out of the elevator and make our way to my apartment in silence. I'm starting to get nervous. I don't know what's going on in his head. Is this what a relationship is like with him? Kinda serious? I was hoping for last Friday part two.

I let him in, and he heads straight for my living room, turning on the light and grabbing the TV remote off the glass coffee table. "You want help making the popcorn?"

My lusty thoughts cool. "No, I got it."

I head to the kitchen. I'm disappointed even though I shouldn't be. He's showing me he's not just into the physical. He wants to do my favorite thing—eat popcorn and watch home renovation shows. I take out a popcorn bag and stick it in the microwave, pressing the popcorn button. I have the latest *Reno Magic* recorded. But if I put that on, will Con notice I'm drooling over the host? Sometimes Clint Owens takes his shirt off to do work outside, and I enjoy it immensely in a solo fashion, if you know what I mean. Would Con want to be part of that?

What am I thinking? I've got the real deal right here. Hot Builder Guy is sitting in my living room. Even better, he's a royal renovator and he says I got him good. Which I think means he's melting around me as much as I'm melting around him, feeling all gooey inside. I don't need the Clint Owens fantasy.

I leave the popcorn and peek into the living room. Connor's arms are spread across the back of the beige sofa, his long legs stretched out and crossed at the ankles.

I can't help myself. He looks so manly spread out across my sofa. I head straight for him.

"No popcorn?" he asks. "I swore I smelled popcorn."

I straddle his lap, my fingers tunneling into the soft hair at the nape of his neck. "I want you."

He gives me a sexy smile, his arms wrapping around me. "I know."

9

Connor

I jerk awake at the sound of Becca's alarm early Saturday morning. She slams it off with one hand and groans. We kept each other up last night. What can I say? The woman wants me bad.

I nuzzle into her neck, and she makes a soft purring sound of contentment before she gasps and shoves me away. She leaps out of bed. "I have to get ready."

I sit up. "Me too."

She holds up a palm. "You can't ride the subway with me to class. We can't be seen together."

"There's tons of people on the subway. No one's going to notice us."

She gives me a stern look, her lips in a tight line. "Con, we need to keep up appearances."

"We will. I'll let you go into the classroom first. No one's going to notice anything."

She nods once and rushes into the bathroom. A few minutes later, she steps out with her toothbrush in her mouth. She pulls it out. "Sit in the back of the room and don't make eye contact."

I toss the covers back and stalk toward her. I'm naked and

her gaze drops to my cock, jerks up to my eyes, and then she quickly heads back to the bathroom.

I follow her in. After she rinses, I wrap my arms around her from behind, kissing her neck. Usually that turns her into a limp noodle, but this time she opens the medicine cabinet and produces a new toothbrush still in its packaging.

"Here," she says, handing it to me.

I take the hint. She wants me minty fresh before I kiss her some more. I brush my teeth and watch in the mirror as she turns on the water for the shower and waits for it to warm. She's tall and willowy, with small perky breasts, a smooth flat stomach, flare of narrow hips, long legs. She reminds me of a fashion model. I think she could've been one if she wasn't so shy and studious. She told me last night while we were talking in the dark that she loved school because she was so good at it, which is part of the reason she's glad to be back in a university setting. I never took school that seriously, knowing I already had a job lined up for me in the family business. If I'd applied myself back then, actually did the work, I might've been good at school too. But the truth is, I enjoy working with my hands, I like a good hard day's work that makes me sweat, and I want to work for the family. I don't regret skipping college, but now I do wish I had a stronger business background.

I make a quick trip back to the bedroom while brushing my teeth and return to the bathroom to rinse and spit. All set. I pull the shower curtain back, joining her.

"Con!"

"Yes, Becca," I say, pulling her into my arms. "I'm minty now." I kiss her and she melts against me. I love the way she does that.

She breaks the kiss. "You have a real issue with boundaries. Promise me you're going to respect boundaries in the classroom. I need you to sit in the back and don't look at me."

I kiss her neck and suck gently on the side. I want her again.

She clings to my shoulders. "C-can you do that?"

I lift my head. "I'll sit in back, but I might have to look at you once in a while. You're right up front and you won't stop talking."

"Be serious."

"So it sounds like roses are out, huh? No grand romantic gestures for my favorite professor?"

Her eyes widen. "Absolutely not."

I smile. "Kidding. Roses are expensive and you know I'm saving for a place." She loves that I'm a saver.

Her lashes flutter down as she stares at my chest. "I know. Another time roses would be romantic. Just not in the classroom."

"You want a guy who does all that girly romantic stuff, don't you?"

Her chin juts out. "And what's wrong with that?"

I run my hands up and down her sides, skimming the sides of her breasts. Her nipples form points. "Absolutely nothing. Now I know the key to Becca."

Her voice is breathy. "Don't do anything inappropriate, okay?"

"Who me?" I caress her breasts, and she moans. "You don't have to worry, I'm the angel of the family."

"I shudder to think of the rest of you."

I pin her against the wall and kiss her long and thorough. I kiss her until her nails dig into my shoulders and her leg lifts, wrapping high around my hip. That's her *I want you so bad* signal. I bite her earlobe and give it a tug. "I bend the rules when it suits me. I don't break them."

She's quiet as I meet her eyes. I study her for a moment. She's definitely turned on but still worried about us. In that moment, I know what she really needs. The key to Becca isn't flowers, it's planning.

I hold her jaw. "I made a plan to spend time with you, and I followed the steps to make it happen."

"Con," she says urgently, lifting her hips.

I slide my hand between us, stroking her. Within moments, she's rocking against me, head thrown back, her grip on my shoulders loosening. Her knees buckle, and I shift her to my front, letting her lean against me, the water running over both of us. I cup her breast, rolling and tugging her nipple while I stroke her, increasing the pace. She's chanting my name, her hips lifting to my rhythm, seeking more of my touch. I love her responses, love her sexy noises. She jerks and then goes off with a sharp cry. I let her ride it out, and then she turns and kisses me urgently, trying to climb my body.

I know what she needs. It's what I need too. I grab the condom I left on the counter and rip it open. "Planning," I tell her.

"Yes," she practically purrs. "Good planning."

She grabs for me the moment I've got it on, and I boost her up, taking her against the wall. "Yes!" she hisses as I drive deep.

I still, trying to regain control. She rocks her hips, grabbing my ass and trying to make me move. "Bec," I say, holding her jaw. "Slow."

I thrust slow and deep, wanting it to last. She kisses me urgently, her hands roaming everywhere, her hips lifting to meet every thrust. Oh God, it feels too good. I still and slide a hand between us, stroking her. She goes wild in my arms, writhing against me. I clamp a hand on her hip, holding her in place. Then I kiss her and that's all it takes. She moans into my mouth, her release squeezing me rhythmically. I let go, pounding into her, driving on and on to oblivion. It crashes into me, an explosion of pleasure that saps my strength. I sag heavily against her.

"Wonderful man!" she exclaims.

I laugh softly. She's so happy after an orgasm, even more so after multiple orgasms. It makes me always want to give her more.

Her fingers run through my hair and she kisses my cheek. "I got you good. What does that mean?"

I lift my head. "I think you know. It's the same way I got you."

She gets serious, searching my face. "We can't screw this up."

I swallow hard. I understand what's at stake, and I'm fully aware I'm the one who pushed for us. If she loses her job because of me, not only will I never forgive myself, she'll never forgive me either. The math is simple—end of her job equals the end of us. It's a calculated risk. But what was the alternative? Ignore the best thing to ever happen to me? I couldn't waste time when I finally met the woman I've been waiting my whole life to meet.

"We won't screw up," I say, gently lifting her off me and setting her in the spray.

"It must be so late," she says, grabbing the soap. "I can't be late."

She quickly washes and leaves. I finish washing alone and turn off the water. There's something special here, and I can only hope it doesn't get ruined by the outside world. Here, just the two of us, things are perfect. For the first time in my life, I feel like I actually need a plan to keep things good. Usually I'd just say whatever happens, happens, but Becca and I, well, that's too important not to be careful.

Becca

I'm back at the lectern, gearing up for my second class. I keep my eyes on my notes, ignoring Con as he strides in and heads to the back of the classroom. I only saw him in my peripheral vision, but I know that body—big and muscular enough to lift a tall woman. *Don't go there.* My cheeks flush hot and I try to focus on anything else.

"Good morning, Ms. Edwards," Mike says cheerfully, taking a seat in the front row. He's wearing a pink button-down shirt and red cords with brown loafers. Pretty dressy for a Saturday morning class.

"Morning, Mike," I say. "Please call me Rebecca."

He stares at me, smiling. First order of business, encouraging everyone to attend Thursday night office hours. I do *not* want to sit through another hour-long Mike lecture. I'll bribe them with cookies if I have to.

"Really enjoyed our discussion on Thursday," Mike says, still smiling at me.

"Glad you got something out of it," I say, smiling at the next few students who come in. I appreciate his enthusiasm, but I don't want anyone to think I'm focusing too much attention on any one student.

Once everyone is seated, I say, "Good morning. I want to make sure you know you're welcome at my office hours Thursday nights from seven to eight p.m. You don't need to have a question, we can just talk shop. Anything I can help you with, whether it's through my own connections or the school's resources, I'm there for you. Plus, we'll have fun. There's homemade cookies."

A few people laugh.

"Hey, I was there last time and there were no cookies," Mike says good-naturedly.

"I forgot them." I lift a finger and declare, "From here on out, there will be cookies. Chocolate chip cookies."

"I'm there!" Mike says.

I catch Con's eye in the back row, and one corner of his mouth lifts in a small smile. I smile back, a flutter in my stomach reminding me of last night and this morning. I tear my gaze away. Mike's staring at me again, but this time his mouth's in a flat line, looking peeved. Did he notice me smiling at Con?

I quickly focus on my notes. "Okay, reminder, your papers are due next week. This is your version of a case study for class discussion. It can be based on a company you previously worked for, currently work for, or just an area of interest to you. Please use last week's case study as an example of format. I want to see background information, what's not working, and some proposed solutions. We'll discuss each one as a class. Now onto today's topic: power and politics in organizations."

I glance up and find everyone staring at their notebooks or laptops, fingers at the ready to record every word. Everyone except Con, who simply listens, his eyes intent on mine. Our gazes lock for an intense moment that makes my pulse race and a flash of heat rush through me. My body knows him, wants him, and it doesn't care that I'm teaching. *Shit.*

I go back to my notes and launch into lecture mode, determined not to get sidetracked with any more long glances. I avoid his eyes for the rest of class. He doesn't participate either. This bothers me, even though I'm sure he's doing it to make me more comfortable. Participation is half the grade for class. I know he's auditing, but he needs to meet class expectations for his own sake and the rest of the group's too.

After class, I take my time getting my stuff together, hoping to catch him near the end of the line of students to talk to him without drawing attention to us. Mike comes up to ask me some questions, which I answer as quickly as I can, my eye on the door. I might catch up with Con on the subway, but maybe not. It was random that our timing worked out last week.

"I'm sorry, Mike," I interrupt as he loops back on another point he made in class today. "I really need to go. We can talk again next week."

"Or at office hours."

"Sure, of course."

He winks and points a finger gun at me. "It's a date."

I stiffen. I really hope he's not getting the wrong idea. "It's an extension of class," I say firmly before heading out the door.

My students have dispersed, and I don't see Con. I don't know why it felt urgent to tell him he could participate in class, but it did, and I'm disappointed. I guess I needed the teacher talk to be in the teacher environment. I'm trying to keep Becca and Con separate from Rebecca and Connor. Hell, maybe I'm just kidding myself with these artificial boundaries. Maybe I had it right the first time. It's foolish to let myself fall when my career's at stake.

I turn the corner at the end of the hall and jump as a large man steps into my path.

"Hey, relax, it's just me." Con leans down to whisper in my ear, "I wanted to wait until everyone else had left to walk you out. You want to stop for coffee before heading back? Somebody kept me up most of the night." He winks, his blue eyes twinkling, and I'm so tempted to throw my arms around him. He's just so warm and so wonderful at making me feel good.

I glance around. There aren't a lot of people nearby, but we're still inside the building, so that means professional teacher boundaries are in order. "Yes to coffee. Let's go."

"You seemed pretty enthusiastic about office hours today. Does that include me?"

"Everyone in class is welcome."

"Are there really going to be homemade chocolate chip cookies?"

I laugh. "Yes. It's a bribe because I don't want a repeat of last week." I quietly fill him in on the boring hour I spent with Mike.

"So he taught you what you already taught him about the case study on coffee."

"Yes."

"For an hour."

"Well, that's how long I'm supposed to be there, but then he wanted to continue the conversation about coffee over coffee. A little too enthusiastic."

He tilts his head. "Is that usual to ask a professor to coffee?"

I adjust the strap of my messenger bag as we head downstairs, and consider the question. "I don't know. I never have as a student, but I guess it happens. It's not really an issue if you're just talking about class."

"Hmm…"

"What? You think he's interested in me?"

"Maybe. I'll keep an eye on him. And I'll be there for office hours."

"No, don't do that. It'll give the wrong impression. I'll explain later." The last thing I want is for Connor to look like an overprotective boyfriend in front of Mike or any of my students. That will be a conversation for once we've left the university campus. "Anyway, I wanted to be sure you know it's important you speak up in class. Participation is half the grade."

"But I don't get a grade. Think of me like the wallpaper. Just there to look good."

I laugh. "Still, it's important to be part of the discussion. Particularly when we break into small groups to discuss the cases. You were the only one who didn't offer an opinion on your case."

"Maybe I didn't have an opinion."

We arrive on the first floor, and I lean close to say quietly, "I don't want you to miss out on the benefit of class because of me. I know I asked you to sit in back and not look at me, but that doesn't mean you have to disappear. Please speak up, let the class know your thoughts. It's okay if you ask questions too. Here's a revision to my previous statement: when we're in class, you may look at me and talk to me, but we'll keep strictly to teacher-student boundaries, and that will make it all go smoothly."

His gaze smolders into mine, his voice husky. "A revision, huh? Now I may look at you." His voice drops to a near whisper. "Talk to you." His words are like a caress. My body hums, sparks firing over my skin.

"Yes," I say softly.

"Good morning, Rebecca," a masculine voice booms.

I jump back from Con and turn to the dean of the business school, my boss. "Good morning, Dean Sears." He's in his fifties with thinning brown hair, wearing his usual brightly colored bow tie—today it's yellow with red polka dots— along with a white dress shirt and dark gray trousers.

"Please call me Robert." He offers Con his hand. "Dr. Robert Sears."

Con shakes his hand. "Connor Rourke, nice to meet you."

Dean Sears smiles and turns to me. "There's a faculty reception for the business school next Saturday I hope you'll be able to attend. You can bring a date." He nods at Connor.

My stomach lurches. Dean Sears assumes we're a couple with the invite. "He's not my date," I blurt. "We're just talking. I just met him. He had a question. I'm single." *Shut up!*

Dean Sears looks at me strangely before saying, "Okay."

"I'd love to go to the faculty reception," I say. "Just me."

"Nothing fancy," Dean Sears says. "Cocktail reception in the lounge."

"Sounds perfect," I say enthusiastically, sweat running down my spine.

"Great. See you then." He heads across the lobby to greet another professor.

I walk on stiff legs toward the exit. This is bad. I shouldn't be seen with Connor too much. Dean Sears could pop into my class at any time and see him sitting there. He'll put two and two together. It's just too risky that something could slip, exposing us.

I glance up at him, and he gives me an understanding look. "I know."

I sigh in relief. He gets it, and he's not hurt that I totally denied all knowledge of him.

I wait until we're safely down the block, heading toward a coffee shop, before saying, "We can't be seen too much together on campus."

"Your workplace, your call," he says. "Can I touch you yet?"

I glance around just in case there's any lingering students. My breath catches as I see Mike watching us from just outside the coffee shop. Did he know I went to this same one last week after class?

"No touching," I say under my breath. "Let's skip coffee." I turn and head toward the subway stop across the street.

Con keeps up with me. "What's wrong?"

"Nothing. I just want to get back."

"Are you freaking out because your boss assumed we were together, and now you think everyone else probably made the same assumption?"

"Not freaking out, but of course it crossed my mind. Do you think everyone assumes we're a couple?"

"I dunno."

I cross the street, frantically trying to remember how many times my gaze caught on his in class today. At least three times. I felt overheated for most of my lecture, my nerves raw and exposed. Did I cover it up as well as I thought?

He goes on. "There's chemistry. Sometimes it's obvious to other people." He shrugs one shoulder. "It's possible no one noticed."

"And it's possible they did."

He exhales sharply. We stop talking while we work our way around some people and reunite on the sidewalk.

"Please don't make me set up another fake blind date just to see you again," he says. "Whether or not you agree to keep seeing me, our chemistry isn't going anywhere. We just have to hide it as best we can in class, that's all."

I want to bang my head against the wall because there's just no easy solution. I can pretend all I want, but the chemistry is a crackling thing between us, even across an entire classroom. Two nights of wild passionate sex has made it impossible for me to keep cool around him. My body will always remember the multiple-orgasm wonderland that is a night with Connor Rourke.

"It's hopeless," I say.

"That's the spirit," he says with a grin.

Once we get on the train, I take an open seat on the long row of seats facing outward, and he drops into the seat next to me.

"You want to do something tonight?" he asks.

My mind immediately turns to dirty thoughts. See? It's just too easy to get wrapped up in him if we're constantly tangled in the sheets. Someone's going to get burned. Me. Besides, I actually do have plans tonight.

"Can't," I say. "I'm going out with my best friend for her birthday." Simone is having a huge birthday bash at a club in the city to celebrate turning thirty, but I leave that out because I don't want him there. I need to talk to her about this whole Connor situation and get her take on it. We've been best friends since kindergarten, and she doesn't hold back when I need her opinion. I desperately need some perspective from someone on the outside. I don't like this constant feeling of wanting to be close to him and needing to keep my distance. It's making me crazy.

"Another time," he says, closing his eyes.

A stab of irritation has me sitting straighter. Okay, I get it. He's tired from last night, and I made us skip coffee to avoid Mike, so now Con wants to nap on the subway ride. It just feels like he's purposely ignoring me because I told him no for tonight. See how crazy this man makes me? I'm never this sensitive.

He takes my hand, entwining our fingers together, and I sigh, leaning my head against his shoulder and closing my eyes. I don't think I can ever resist him. Everything with Connor is so complicated. Why am I torturing myself like this?

10

Becca

That night I check in with the young brunette woman wearing a headset outside the club for Simone's birthday party bash. "Hi, I'm Becca Edwards."

She checks the list, finds my name, and speaks into the headset before smiling at me. "Go on in."

I follow the red carpet runner to the glass front door, which a bulky-with-muscles bouncer opens for me. I step into the club to a thumping bass beat that vibrates the floor. Another man in a suit with an earpiece greets me, taking my coat and directing me upstairs. A couple of tough-looking guys also wearing earpieces stand nearby. Why all the security? My best friend is Simone Rivera, internationally famous pop star. To me she'll always be the girl I found crying in the coat closet in kindergarten because her shirt had a hole in it and the other girls were calling her holy Simone. She was poor and even at that age was aware of the fact that her clothes were from the thrift store. I told her we could be twins, which meant we could wear each other's clothes. I don't know where I got that from. I'm blond with light blue eyes and pale skin; she's brunette with deep brown eyes and golden tan skin. I'm tall; she's average height. Obviously no one would mistake us for twins. But she happily wore some of the shirts and dresses that I'd outgrown. They were still in great shape because it was just me at home—no siblings—and I wasn't hard on my clothes. Anyway, we bonded and now, twenty-five years later, we're still close. I just don't get to see her as much as I'd like. It used to be hard to meet up because of all the travel involved with my job, but in the past two years, it's been because of her job. She finally made it big like I always knew she would.

Upstairs, there's a packed dance floor and people lounging around the edges of it on cushioned red cubes. I check around for her and notice a few private booths off to the left. I bet she's there.

I head over and there she is, tucked into a booth with a bunch of people I don't know. As soon as she spots me, she screams and throws her hands in the air. "Becca! My twin!" Her long dark brown hair is up in a cute high ponytail. She gestures for some of the other people in the booth to shift out of her way, and hurries over to me, as much as she can hurry in a skintight silver sequined minidress with knee-high white platform boots. My little black dress with black pumps is so blah in comparison.

She grabs me in a monster hug and kisses my cheek. She pulls back to look at me, her hands still on my shoulders, and grins. "How's it feel to be thirty?"

I smile and say in a teasing voice, "I wouldn't know. I've still got seven months left in my twenties."

"Impossible. We're twins!"

"Happy birthday, twin." I give her the gift bag. She's tough to buy for because she basically has everything she could possibly want with the gobs of money she's raking in.

She leads me to a small roped-off area in the corner with a square table and four chairs. "I saved this spot for us so we could catch up. I haven't seen you in *forever*." She takes a seat, drags another chair right next to hers for me, and then peeks inside her gift bag, pulling out a pack of cherry Twizzlers. "Oh, I miss these. Not on my healthy tour diet."

I nudge her shoulder and say in a singsong voice, "Well, if you don't want them, I know someone who does." It's a favorite quote of ours from *The Simpsons* when Homer gives Marge the gift he really wants—a bowling ball with his name on it.

She laughs, rips open the package and offers me a Twizzler before biting down on her own. She pulls the next gift out of the bag—a small box—and holds it up. "Mmph." She hands me her half-eaten licorice stick so she can use both hands to open the box. "I love it!" She puts on her new bracelet, beaming at it.

It's a silver bracelet with three interlocking rings of dull gray, silver, and gold. "It's supposed to represent the past, present, and future. The gray is past, silver in the middle is the present, and gold is the future. It's a reminder to live in the present and plan for the future, no looking back to the gray past. Seemed appropriate with the wave you've been riding. I hope you're soaking up everything that's great about the now."

Her eyes shine with unshed tears. "Oh, Bec. This couldn't have come at a better time. I've been worried about the next album, whether I can explore something new and still please fans, and this is a great reminder." She strokes the silver ring of the bracelet. "I really do want to live in the moment and not worry so much about the future."

A waiter stops by, and Simone orders us some champagne.

"Okay, tell me everything," she says after the waiter leaves. "How's teaching going? Do you love it as much as you thought you would?"

"I like it, but..." I take a deep breath. "Something very weird and entirely inappropriate has popped up, and I just don't know what to do about it."

Her brows shoot up. "You, inappropriate."

"Yes."

She smacks my shoulder. "Tell me!"

I fill her in on meeting Connor and my unusual one-night stand with him, which turned out to be more.

"Get it, girl," she says, nodding. "Didn't I tell you to have some fun after Oliver Dullard?" My ex's last name is Bullard, but Simone called him Dullard for obvious reasons. She called him that even *before* we broke up, and I probably should've taken her assessment more seriously.

She smiles brightly. "So what's wrong with having fun with this guy?"

I shake my head, embarrassed over the situation I'm in. I know it's wrong, yet I keep seeing him. She'd be shocked at the way I've compromised my ethical integrity all because of my out-of-control lust. It's really not like me at all. Okay, it's not just lust. I like him. A lot. He's so warm. I love the way his eyes crinkle with his smile and his laid-back acceptance of just about anything I say. I don't think he'd ever call me an ice queen just because I'm not smiling. And I feel comfortable with him, really relaxed, which doesn't always happen easily for me. It's only been a little over a week, but I can already feel myself falling for him. Stupid tender heart.

I sigh. "I'm veering too far from my life plan."

"Hey, you know I don't knock the life plan. It's smart and that kind of thinking—Becca thinking—is how I got where I am today."

I sit a little straighter, proud that my planning skills were so successful for her.

She goes on. "But sometimes you just gotta let loose. Speaking of…" She beams at the waiter who just arrived with our champagne. He removes the cork with a pop, and Simone claps.

After we each have a glass of champagne in hand, we clink glasses and sip.

"Okay, so let me see if I understand this correctly," she says. "You feel like you did something weird and inappropriate by having a one-night stand?" She smacks my arm. "And why wasn't I notified immediately?"

"Ow." I rub my arm and shoot her a dark look. "It got complicated fast and I was too embarrassed."

Her eyes widen. "Did he turn out to be your cousin or something?"

"No!" I stare at the table. "He's my student."

She squeaks, and I face her. Her hand is over her mouth, her eyes huge. See, I knew it was bad.

"I know," I say miserably. "It's awful. I didn't know he was my student until he showed up in my classroom the morning after."

She drops her hand. "How old is he?"

"He's got to be late twenties at least. It's grad school, and he's all man, filled out with muscle, little crinkles by his eyes when he smiles, a confident take-charge attitude."

"Oh my God, Bec! You're really into this guy!" Her voice carries loud enough for the entire club to hear, probably the entire city block.

I attempt to cool my full-body blush by tossing back my champagne and then cough as the bubbles go down the wrong way.

Simone slaps me on the back a few times. "How do you not know his age? Don't you research your guys before you decide to be with them?"

I wipe at the corners of my eyes. "I did Google him. Somehow I got so caught up in the fact that he's a prince I missed his age."

"He's a prince too?" she whisper-shouts.

I lower my palm in a gesture for her to keep it down. "Yes, and a builder."

She wiggles the fingers of both hands toward herself. It's her major announcement gesture, her *tell me everything* gesture, her *look closely at my face before I smack you* gesture. It's all encompassing and so her. "So you're telling me you basically met your fantasy times two."

"Yes!" I'm glad she gets it, even if I am doing the wrong thing. There's some sound logical fantasy impulses at play here. Is that where the passion comes from? Con's words come back to me. *Becca, here's the facts. We have insane chemistry.* That means it's a two-way street, and I don't think he has a teacher fantasy. Wait, does he? Gah. What is this thing between us and why? I feel like if I could just understand it better without all my confusing emotions, then I wouldn't be so worked up all the time.

"A royal and a builder," Simone says with a smile. "It's like you dreamed him up."

"I know. A royal renovator. It's perfect." I frown. "Except for the teacher-student part. What should I do? I really want this job, and I don't want to be accused of anything inappropriate. I might never get a job in academia again. Even worse, my dad is good friends with my boss, Dean Sears. They were friends in college."

She pours me another glass of champagne. "Wow. That is a pickle."

A couple of guys approach to ask her to dance. "Later, promise!" she says with a smile. "I'm catching up with my twin."

They give me a strange look before heading over to the dance floor. No one ever believes we're twins.

My mind goes back to Connor, as it always does in a moment of quiet. Is it wrong to keep seeing him?

How can I resist him? My track record in that regard is a total fail.

Simone leans close, lowering her voice. "How's the sex?"

I've had enough champagne to admit it. Plus, it's Simone. "Best I've ever had."

She puts her arm around me. "Here's what you're going to do. Keep seeing this guy, keep having the best sex of your life, and keep it all secret. It'll make it even hotter. Your secret royal renovator lover."

I smile at first, but then it wavers. "I don't know. It still feels like there's too much risk for me."

"Drink more champagne."

I shake my head, laughing. We both take a drink. She grabs my purse off the side of my chair and hands it to me. "Invite him here. I want to meet him."

My heart kicks into overdrive. "How's that going to help anything?"

"I'll see you together and then I'll know if he's worth the risk."

"Of losing my job? No man is worth that risk, especially if it closes teaching to me forever. And you know my parents. They'd disown me and they'd never accept him. The shame would be too much to bear."

"Bec."

"What?" I ask miserably, lost in my conflicting emotions and inconvenient morals.

"You deserve to be happy. That's all I care about. Now invite him over."

I exhale sharply. "All you'll see is that we have chemistry. I need to think clearly when he's not around so I can *figure this thing out*. This needs to be a rational decision completely separate from whatever happens to me when I'm in his vicinity. I lose my good sense, Simone."

She holds out her palm. "Phone, *por favor*."

She knows how much I appreciate good manners in any language, but I stay strong. "You're not calling him."

"Come on, it'll be fun. He'll like getting a call from Simone Rivera. Everyone does."

I slowly shake my head. "Ah, hello! Remember when you told me to let you know when you're getting too caught up in the hype?" I put my hand on her arm. "Huge fandom, suck-up staff. The hype is all over you right now."

"Which is why I asked you to join my people as business manager. Plus your mad skillz."

She fired her business manager last month after a huge sexual harassment scandal broke about him with another very young client. I'd already secured my teaching position at the time with high hopes of a new career, or I would've given her job offer serious thought. After my burnout, I'll admit the idea of moving to LA and traveling with her when she needed me to was more than I could handle, but I'm in a better place now.

She gets serious, speaking in an urgent tone. "I'm incorporating, you know. And the truth is, I need you, Bec. Will you please at least think about it? I trust you like no one else."

I take a deep breath. I want to be there for her. It could be an incredible opportunity, a lucrative one too, but I'd have to give up my life here. That means seeing my family a lot less. We're close. And I'd have to say goodbye to Connor. No way he'd leave his family business. But that's planning on a hypothetical. I don't know for sure I have a future with Connor;

things are still so new between us. I can't completely close the door on this opportunity.

I give her arm a squeeze. "I need to finish out my semester, but I'll give it serious consideration."

"Yay!" She throws her arms around me and kisses my cheek. "Now, please call Connor. I've got to meet this guy to see if he's worth all the angst."

"You know, if I worked for you, I probably wouldn't see him anymore. Long distance never works."

She holds up her new jangly bracelet and points to the gold band. "That's the future. You and me, we're living in the present. Besides, you've still got the rest of the semester. So, at the moment, you're into a guy who's got you breaking all the rules. I think this is the first time you ever broke your five-date rule, isn't it?"

"Yes," I admit.

"I'm only in town for a week, and it's important I meet him. You can't expect me to give you good advice without seeing you together."

Living in the moment. Didn't I just tell her how important that was? I set my small purse on the table and stare at it. *Should I call him? Maybe it would help if Simone met him.* My pulse jumps, nerves skittering over my skin. "I'm not calling him."

"At least show me his picture. Please tell me you got a picture of your prince."

I smile, pulling out my phone and showing her the picture of Connor in a tux with his brothers on Villroy Island for Dylan's wedding. She snags the phone out of my hand and turns her back to me.

"Simone! Give that back!"

"I just want to see. Rourke. Oh, hey, small world. I met Princess Emma and her husband, Jackson, at a party in London. Super nice and so talented. Both of them. Hello, this is Simone Rivera. I was wondering if you'd like to join me and Becca at my birthday party?"

"Simone!" I lunge for my phone, and she leaps up and backs away, holding me off with one hand.

"Yes, it really is Simone Rivera the singer." She launches into one of her hits. "I'm on fire for your love…what? I'm on Becca's phone because she's here with me—ah!" She yanks her arm out of my grip. "Sorry, your girlfriend is really strong."

I cover my face with my hands. I never said I was his girl-friend. We haven't put a label on whatever this thing is. This is so freaking embarrassing.

Simone pulls one of my hands away from my face and gives me my phone back. "He wants to talk to you."

"Hello," I say into the phone, glaring at her. "Sorry about that."

Connor's deep voice warms me immediately. "Your best friend is Simone Rivera? How did that happen?"

"We grew up together." I add loudly, "Which is why she thinks she can just butt into my life."

She grins and takes a seat, sucking her champagne through a licorice straw. She's immediately surrounded by a group of people wishing her happy birthday and exclaiming over her. They were probably just waiting for me to step away. Life of a diva. I'm happy for her—no one deserves it more than she does after all her hard work—even though I'm irritated by her tricky tactics.

I step farther away for privacy. "Were you busy?"

"Just watching the Yanks. It's a tie game."

"Oh, well, I'll let you get back to the game."

"Bec, it's a little strange that your famous friend called to invite me to her birthday party. What's going on?"

I sigh. "She wants to meet you."

"Why?"

"Because I told her about us."

"Yeah, what did you say?" He sounds eager to know.

"I'd rather not share. Girl talk."

"That sounds ominous."

"I'm having an ethical dilemma."

"I hate when that happens. Give me the address and I'm there."

My pulse thrums through my veins. This could be a

disaster—him, me, Simone. The situation is too far out of my control. "I'm at a club in the city. So not your scene."

"Address, please."

I give it to him since he was so polite. Dammit. The *please* gets me every time.

"See ya soon," he says and disconnects.

I walk over and pretend strangle Simone.

She laughs. "You're welcome!"

11

───

My heart thunders as Connor strides toward me and Simone at our private table in the corner. I knew the moment he arrived because security sent the message to Simone. She immediately sent everyone else away from the table. I've been practically vibrating in anticipation ever since.

She speaks under her breath. "He hauls his ass all the way from Brooklyn, leaving the Yanks in a tie game. Girl, he's into you. And fi-i-ine. Mmm-hmm."

I leap from my seat, fueled by the adrenaline of anticipating him for the last hour.

I meet him halfway, my breath quickening as our gazes lock. *He's here.* All of my angst over him vanishes. My brain seems to take a hike when I'm close to him, a welcome relief. "Thank you for coming."

He dips his head, kissing my cheek. "Good to see ya. Think I'll pass best-friend inspection?" He holds his arms out, inviting me to check him out. He's gorgeous, sexy, intoxicating. I want him so freaking bad.

"Your blue shirt brings out your eyes," I say by way of covering up my intense lust. He's wearing a long-sleeved button-down shirt open at the collar, exposing the notch between his collarbones that I've tasted. A low ache of desire builds as I take in his slim waist in belted dark gray trousers with black dress shoes. Such a gorgeous man.

He tips my chin up. "Thank you."

"Everything brings out your eyes. They're this incredible blue," I blurt.

He smiles, his eyes lighting up, those tiny crinkles forming around them. "I like your dress. You look beautiful."

"Thanks. How old are you?"

He drops an arm over my shoulders and kisses my temple. "Google didn't tell you?"

I'd like to put some righteous indignation into my voice, but can't manage it. The truth is, I tried to do thorough research on him only to get caught up in how handsome he looked in his tux. "I'm asking *you*."

He shifts us, walking with me toward Simone. He recognized her, as just about everyone does nowadays. She gives me a big smile and a double thumbs-up. My cheeks flame. Could she be more obvious? And it's a little early to give the thumbs-up. He just got here. She hasn't even spoken to him yet.

"I'm twenty-eight," he says.

"That's good."

"Is it? How old did you think I was?"

"Around my age, but I just wanted to be sure. I like knowing all the facts. Simone asked." I'm babbling because I'm basically about to put the whole teacher-student situation up for Simone's inspection. I know it looks bad, and I know it's risky. It's my job on the line with tremendous potential fallout both personally and professionally.

Simone rushes over to us, giving him her full-wattage pop-star smile. "Hi! I'm Simone. So great to meet you."

He takes his arm off me to shake her hand. "You too. I'm Connor."

"I know." She smiles, looking from me to Connor. "Come, have a seat." She gestures to the table. We follow her there. She tells us to sit in the two close-together seats, where she and I were sitting, and then pulls a third seat over next to my other side. Now all three of us are sitting on one side of the table—me in the middle. So cozy and comfortable. Not.

An awkward silence settles in. Except for the loud club music.

Simone picks up her phone. "What can I get you, Connor? We're having champagne, but there's a full bar if you want something else."

He politely requests a Brooklyn IPA, and I feel all mushy inside. Surely, Simone will notice his fine manners and see that's a point in his favor for more than just the fact that he's probably the sexiest guy I've ever been with. I really want her approval of him. Maybe I'm just trying to rationalize my desire to be with him.

After she puts in the order by text, she smiles brightly at him. "So, Becca tells me you're a princely builder."

"Just a builder," he says. "Not princely."

"He's royal by blood," I put in. "He just likes to keep it more of a secret thing."

Simone hides a smile as she lifts her glass of champagne. "I like secret things." She sips her drink, her eyes sparkling playfully at me. She did tell me to keep this thing with Connor secret.

"Secrets can be a double-edged sword," Connor says.

"Agreed," I say.

Three guys approach the table, trying to get Simone on the dance floor. She smiles at them. "I'll get there, I promise! Right now I'm catching up with my girl and her new guy."

One of the guys snaps a birthday selfie with her and they walk away.

Simone doesn't miss a beat, leaning toward Connor to ask, "What other secrets are you keeping?"

I lean back, away from the close middle between them.

"Nothing," Connor says.

I push Simone back. "Chill."

"I just think it's an interesting thing to say," Simone says. "Like he has personal experience with secrets."

I turn to Connor in question. *Is there something I should know?*

He gives my hand a squeeze. "My dad kept his relationship with my mom a secret because she was a commoner and he already had a marriage arranged for him. Then when his dad was on his death bed and it was time for my dad to step up as king, marry his queen, and carry on for the kingdom, he finally admitted he'd been secretly seeing my mom and wanted her for his bride. Some say the shock of that is what got him exiled with nothing but the shirt on his back."

Simone's eyes are huge, her jaw gaping. She turns to me for my reaction. I'm just as surprised to hear it was all a secret. That didn't come up in my research.

"That's so romantic!" Simone gushes, squeezing his arm.

He lifts one shoulder. "My dad always says he did it to marry the best woman in the world."

"Oh wow," she says on a sigh.

"That's beautiful," I murmur.

His beer arrives and he takes a long swallow, the Adam's apple in his thick neck moving up and down. I subtly lean closer, breathing him in—ocean, sunshine, and male sex appeal. He's like sex on the beach. The cocktail *and* the real deal. *Delicious.*

Simone smiles at him. "I love your parents' story. How about you, though? Any bad breakups in the past?"

Connor glances sideways at me before saying, "No."

"Expand," Simone says, a note of steel in her voice.

"No bad breakups," he says evenly.

"Did you dump them, or they dumped you?" she asks.

"Simone!" I protest. "You're getting too personal."

"Personal is asking how he feels about you," she says with a devilish smile. "See how I didn't do that?"

Connor opens his mouth, shuts it, and takes a drink of beer.

"You're making him uncomfortable," I say. "Enough with the questions."

"Sorry, you're right," Simone says. "Come on, it's my birthday. Let's dance." She pulls me out of my chair. "Please, Bec, I want to have some fun and I want you to be part of it. You too, Connor."

I turn to him in question.

He stands. "Sure."

We head over to the dance floor. Simone throws her hands in the air, dancing her way to the center. She's immediately surrounded by a circle of admirers. These people have all been vetted, so I don't worry about her safety. The song is another thumping bass beat, and, this close to the speakers, I feel it like a heartbeat pressing in on my body.

I start to dance and Con snakes an arm around my waist, holding me loosely but close enough that we're touching as I move. He matches my rhythm, and desire unfurls through me, my limbs heavy and loose. My mind clears. There's nothing but the primal satisfaction of my body close to his. Time ceases to exist. His hands skate up and down my sides. It's electric. I wrap my arms around his neck, and we're dancing, barely, pressed up against each other. It's like foreplay, his eyes smoldering into mine, and we just keep going and going, dancing our way closer and closer to the flame.

Soon, his body says, *naked time soon*.

And mine says, *yes, yes, yes*.

A long while later, Simone grabs my arm. "Quick thing, twin."

"Huh? What is it?"

She pulls me off the dance floor, saying to Connor over her shoulder, "We'll meet you at our table."

He lifts a hand and heads back to the table. I watch him go with his confident stride, his big shoulders and broad back retreating from me when I want nothing more than to feel them under my palms. We should go back to my place soon. I can't even believe how much I want this man. It's insane, out of control, a craving I can't deny.

Simone stops a distance from the dance floor, close to the stairs, and points downstairs over the glass rail. "It's Clint Owens. I invited him for you and didn't think he was coming. He never responded, and I heard he was away on a shoot. I'll introduce you, and then you go back to Connor. Whatever you do, don't let Connor see you drooling over Clint."

"What! Clint Owens is here! For me!" I'm hyperventilating. He's my idol, my fantasy man from my favorite home renovation show, *Reno Magic*. We've had many orgasm-filled nights together over the years. Solo orgasms, but still, he played an important imaginary role.

"Yes." She grips me by the shoulders. "*Breathe*. Celebrities don't like when people lose their shit over them at a private party. Just be your polite self."

I nod vigorously and then turn to stare at the familiar tousled brown hair and granite jaw on the sexy builder I've been fantasizing about for, oh, *forever* as he heads upstairs, closer and closer.

OH MY GOD, IT'S CLINT OWENS!!!

My breath quickens, my heart racing, jaw gaping. I can't believe he's really here. Clint Owens in person! My fantasy come to life.

As he gets closer, I realize his handsome face is impossibly more handsome in person. I'm frozen in place, in total awe. He's dressed in a black suit, no tie, his white shirt open to mid-chest, exposing his defined pecs and tribal tattoo. My mind flashes to my go-to fantasy where I magically step into the *Reno Magic* show, and Clint Owens and I are hammering something together and then suddenly we're hammering each other up against the wall. *Oh God, I'm throbbing.*

"Clint!" Simone exclaims. "I didn't think you could make it. What a nice surprise!"

He smiles his million-dollar smile, his teeth glowing white in the dim light of the club. "How could I resist you, Simone? And when you told me your friend was such a fan of the show, I had to make the trip. Besides, we wrapped up early on a house in South Carolina. Short flight and here I am."

"Yay!" she says.

"Happy birthday," he says, giving her an air kiss. His gaze lands on me. "Is this her?"

I blink a few times and lick my dry lips. Was I standing here with my mouth hanging open the whole time?

Simone nudges me. "This is her, my best friend from way, way back, Becca. And, Becca, you know Clint, of course, from your fave show, but here he is in person."

I take in his brown eyes with thick lashes, sparkling knowingly at me. It's almost like he knows me the way I know him. My knees go weak, my hands trembling.

Clint. Owens. Here.

Simone nudges me again.

"Big fan," I blurt. It's all the words I can manage.

He takes my hand between his two large, surprisingly soft hands. "Becca, so nice to meet a fan. Which season is your favorite?"

Clint Owens is touching me. I can't move, can't look away. His full lips are so sensual, even stretched into a smile. *Clint Owens is smiling at me.*

"I'm pretty sure she likes all of them," Simone answers for me.

"I like all of them," I echo in a breathy voice.

"Well, that's great to hear," he says, smiling in his winning, Clint Owens way.

He likes what I'm saying, so I say more as if in a trance, caught up in the phenomenal aura of the charming host and sexy builder who's seen me through many a lonely, sex-deprived night. "I've watched all five seasons, but I think it's the more recent ones where you've taken on more of the work solo that've really been incredibly awesome." *Because you're shirtless.*

Simone pipes up. "I'm so glad Becca finally got a chance to meet you and let you know how much she likes your show."

He lifts my hand and kisses the back of it, his eyes burning into mine. My breath catches, my brain floating away on a dream. I'm having an out-of-body experience. It's magic. *Reno Magic.*

"Come with me," Simone says, looping her arm through his. "I've got some other people I'd like you to meet."

"Later," he tells Simone, and then he turns to me with a charming, sexy host smile. "Becca, would you like to dance?"

"Dance," I echo blankly, reality rushing in. We don't dance in my fantasies. I blink and look around. Where's Con? I was dancing with him.

He chuckles. "Yes, dance." And then Clint Owens puts a

hand on the small of my back and leads me to the dance floor. He's not as tall as I thought he was on TV. I'm a little bigger than him in my heels.

I don't want to be rude, so I decide one dance won't hurt. I keep my eye out for Con and finally spot him at the private table in the corner, where we were before. I wave him over. He stands and walks toward me, his expression stormy. *Uh-oh.*

Suddenly Clint pulls me close, his eyes heavy-lidded, locked on mine.

Clint Owens wants to hammer me.

Mind blown.

"Can I cut in?" a deep voice barks.

I whirl. "Con! Hi! I was hoping you'd join me."

His jaw is tight, his shoulders somehow wider like he's in battle stance. "Hi."

Ooh, this is bad. I gesture toward my fantasy man, who's backed away from me. "Con, this is Clint Owens from *Reno Magic*. Simone told him I'm a fan, so he asked me to dance."

Con shakes his hand brusquely before saying in a voice that brooks no argument, "She's with me."

Clint jerks his chin and shifts to another part of the dance floor. He's immediately surrounded by young, beautiful writhing women. *Goodbye, Clint Owens. Until we meet again on TV.*

Con takes my hand and guides me away from the dance floor toward a private booth that's empty since everyone flocked to the dance floor to be near Clint Owens. I think Simone is on the dance floor too. Obviously he's the bigger draw with the women.

I settle on the cushioned banquette, my eyes drifting back toward Clint Owens—it's so hard to believe he's here in real life—when Con suddenly hauls me all the way to the center of the seat right up against him, thigh to thigh.

I turn to him, still enthralled with the turn of events. "Can you believe Clint Owens from *Reno Magic* is here?"

His eyes narrow. "Why do you say it like *he's* magic?"

I tilt my head. "Are you jealous?"

He looks over my shoulder. Probably shooting jealous laser beams of death at poor unsuspecting Clint Owens. "Why would I be jealous?"

I glance back at the dance floor, and Con cups my jaw and turns me back to him. He kisses me roughly, his fingers gripping my hair. Lust spears through me like lightning. I go damp between the legs, my nipples in aching points, all of me dying for more of his touch. I moan deep in my throat, and then I'm lost in the overwhelming pleasure of a man who wants to claim me as his own, thoroughly, completely his.

When he finally lets me up for air, we're both breathing hard. He shifts, dropping his hold on me.

"Tell me why I'd be jealous," he says quietly.

I'm so turned on I want to climb on top of him and grind away. *I need, I need—*

"Bec."

I meet his intense blue eyes. He wants me to be his, only his. That means something. "You don't need to be jealous. I'm here with you."

"You sure looked excited to be with him."

I bite my lower lip. "Okay, I get why you're jealous. I have a thing for builders. You're a builder, he's a builder. And I might've gone fangirl over meeting my—*him* in person."

"Your what? You were about to say my *what*?"

"Nothing." I move to kiss him, but he pulls back.

"I could only see you partly in profile, but what I did see looked like you were about to kiss him. Is that accurate?"

My cheeks flame. "Kiss him? I wasn't about to kiss him."

"You were very close on the dance floor, and he was looking at you with clear lust in his eyes. What am I supposed to think?"

"It's not like that. We just met."

"Uh-huh. Is he the reason I got a late invitation? You were hoping to meet up with him?"

"No! We really did just meet. I'm, uh, a big fan of the show. I had no idea he'd be here. Simone invited him and—" I stare at the table, tracing a scar in the wood "—and you, and now it's just *weird*."

Lusty worlds colliding.

Though only one of them is real. Obviously I prefer a real man in my life to a fantasy one on TV! It's not like I'm going to sleep with Clint Owens, even if I do fantasize about it.

He cups my jaw, lifting my face to his before kissing me in his thorough drugging way. I'm so glad he's kissing me again.

He breaks the kiss. "Tell me why it's weird." His kisses turn me into a puddle of need. I suspect he knows that because he does it again.

"Con."

He kisses me longer this time. "Tell me."

My hand goes to his chest, clutching his shirt to keep him close. "More, please."

He kisses along the line of my jaw and gives my earlobe a tug between his teeth. His words run hot over my skin. "Have you been with him?"

"No, I swear, he's just a fantasy."

He meets my eyes, studying me for a long moment. "A fantasy?"

I look away. It's kinda embarrassing to talk about my fantasy man when he's right there. Especially to my real man.

"Bec?"

"Yeah?"

"Look at me."

I meet his eyes, praying he won't ask exactly what I do in my fantasy with Clint Owens. That's private.

His brows knit together. "Before, you invited me back to your place to watch *Reno Magic* so you could watch your fantasy man. Is that right?"

"Uh, not exactly."

"Exactly how was it?"

I go on the defensive. "You invited yourself back to my place, remember? I just happened to have the latest show recorded and thought you might enjoy it too from a builder's perspective."

"While you enjoyed it as a way to get off?"

"Shh!" I glance around, but no one is nearby. The dance floor is packed with the two celebrities, who are now dancing with each other. *Simone and Clint Owens. Wow, they'd make beautiful babies.*

"Do you still watch him to get off?"

I put a hand over his mouth and hiss, "Stop saying get off."

He pulls my hand away. "It's embarrassing when you meet your fantasy man while your real man is around."

Wow, really nailed that one.

"He's just here," I say lamely. Can I help it if my mind immediately went into Clint Owens fantasy mode, as it's been trained to do for the past several years? There's a well-worn neural pathway from Clint Owens to orgasm.

"I'm going to talk to him." He slides out of the booth, and I hurry to follow him as best I can, but my dress keeps sticking to the velvet cushioning. He mostly lifted me when I first sat in the center of the long seat.

I catch up to him and grab his arm. "Con, wait. Just stay with me."

"I wanna get to know the competition."

"There's no competition, I swear."

His jaw is tight. "Then come with me and let me see how you are with him up close."

"You're just trying to embarrass me. Forget it. Do what you want. I'm going to dance with Simone."

He stalks off and I stand there, frozen in place, watching as he says something to Clint Owens that has him leaving the dance floor. They go off to the side to talk.

I hurry over toward Simone, waving my hands above the circle of dancers surrounding her. "Twin!" Luckily, I'm tall and she spots me, dragging me into the center with her.

"Bad news," I tell her.

"What? Speak up!"

"Bad news! Con went to talk to Clint Owens!"

"Leave the men to alpha it out." She grabs my hand and spins me around. "Dance with the birthday girl. You only turn thirty once."

"What if they fight?" I ask as she twirls me around again.

"There's security. Stop worrying so much. You'll probably have sweaty makeup sex!"

I flush and shift to spy on the two men. They're in a small overlook jutting out from the dance floor. Con looks serious as he talks. They're sort of squared off, legs spread shoulder-width apart. Clint Owens is glossy and styled. Con is rugged and real. Also, taller by a few inches. I'm dying to know what Con's saying. What if he's informing Clint Owens that he's my fantasy man? How can I ever live it down?

Simone yanks me toward her and dances in a circle around me. *Oh, fine. I'll dance with the birthday girl.*

Approximately three exhausting dances later, Con appears on the dance floor and jerks his chin for me to follow. I do, and we end up back at Simone's reserved table in the corner since the private booths are filled again.

He sits next to me and drops an arm over my shoulders. "Turns out Clint isn't a contractor. He's an actor. That's why he's only recently been doing more of the renovation work. He has a coach on set who tells him what to do." He sounds smug.

"So that was your goal? Ruin my fantasy man for me?"

"Nah. I just wanted to find out what he was about. Now we know."

I'm mad, but also kinda happy that he cares enough to be so worked up over my celebrity crush. I think Simone's right —Con's really into me.

I turn to him. "That's worse than jealous. It's petty."

"I'll admit to jealous. Not petty. If I were petty, I would've broken his nose for kissing your hand."

"Con!"

"Okay, fine. I wouldn't punch him, but I definitely wouldn't have been polite."

I lift my chin. "Just because I went fangirl over my fantasy come to life doesn't mean you need to go caveman. Nothing was going to happen."

His hand wraps around the back of my neck, stroking the sensitive skin with his thumb. "Just know this, *I'm* now your fantasy builder man."

Ooh, this is even better. I can actually act out my longtime fantasies. I rub his chest, enjoying the warmth of his hard muscles. "My fantasy builder man takes off his shirt and does real reno work."

He nips my lower lip. "And where do you come in?"

"I help."

He laughs. "You help?"

"Yes, why is that funny? I help with my hammer."

His eyes dance with amusement, and he kisses me again. "Then what?"

"Then things progress from there."

He cups my face in both his hands. "You're adorable when you're blushing. Show me later."

"Only if you pass the builder test. It has to look authentic to fulfill the fantasy."

"Oh, it'll be authentic."

"Con?"

"Yeah."

"I'd like to go now. I need to know if you can pass the builder test. Otherwise..." I tilt my head toward the dance floor as though Clint Owens is a real possibility.

Con plucks me right out of my seat, and I squeak in surprise. "Time to prove myself." He hauls me against him and kisses me passionately.

Time for sweaty makeup sex. With tools!

He breaks the kiss, grinning. "We'd better go to my place, where there's actual tools."

"Oh, yeah," I breathe.

He chuckles, takes my hand, and guides me out. We stop to say goodbye to Simone, and she hugs both of us, which means he's got the Simone stamp of approval. She's not a big hugger despite all her loud enthusiastic friendliness.

"I expect to see you again, Connor!" she says.

"Sounds good," he says.

I feel Clint Owens's eyes on me and catch Con giving him a jaunty salute. My former fantasy man turns away, pretending not to notice. The salute is like the polite-guy version of *fuck off*. Con being the polite guy.

"Simone likes you," I say when we reach the sidewalk outside.

"Best-friend stamp of approval," he says, taking my hand as we walk to the subway stop. "Glad I passed the test."

"It wasn't a test."

"Yeah, it was."

"Okay, a little bit. I was conflicted, but…"

He glances over at me. "But…"

"But I want to be with you, so if we keep it a secret, it should be okay."

"So that's what she meant about secrets."

"Yes."

"Okay, but that's the only secret, got it? Anything you want to tell me about?"

"No, I don't have any secrets."

"Me either. So now we can get back to this builder fantasy starring me, a guy who actually knows how to use tools because I'm a real builder."

"I can't wait!"

He chuckles and hugs me tight. And, for one shining moment, I forget every doubt and worry I have about us.

12

———

Connor

I take Becca back to my place for the first time. Compared to hers, it's extremely sparse, so I'm thinking she's not going to be too impressed. I've only lived here a month. There's a black leather sofa with a coffee table, end table, and flat-screen TV in the living room, and a king-sized bed, dresser, and a couple of nightstands in the bedroom. That's it.

She takes a quick look around my living room. "Where do you keep your tools?"

I stifle a laugh. "Bathroom closet."

I go to get my toolbox, and she follows me. How did I find the one woman turned on by everything about me? It's not like working in construction or being part of the outcast royal family has ever played in my favor before. And definitely not the combination of those things. I'm just a regular guy.

I set the toolbox on the dresser in my bedroom. I figure I'll hang that full-length mirror I've been meaning to put up. It's late and I don't want to disturb the neighbors. One nail in the wall and Becca's all mine.

"What're you going to build?" she asks.

Gotta love her enthusiasm. If she actually wanted to see me build, she'd have to show up at my work. I've got to be creative to make this fantasy happen tonight after I got a little worked up over her and Clint. But I read the lust in his eyes for her, and Becca was acting very strange, the way she kept swaying toward him. She's usually much more reserved and, well, upright.

I open the toolbox, and she peers inside. "I'm renting, so I can't go crazy renovating, but I did want to put up a mirror in here."

"Okay, I'll watch."

"Is this how your fantasy usually works?"

"Well…" She twirls a lock of her hair. "Since there's no secrets between us…promise not to laugh."

I wrap my arms around her waist. "I won't laugh."

She meets my eyes and licks her lips. "You do your hammering work, shirtless, and then I show up to help." She rests her hands on my chest.

"So you can admire my muscles, I assume." Or Clint Owens's muscles. I can never watch *Reno Magic* again.

She strokes my chest, her eyes glued to it. "Yes, but then when we get close to each other, it's so hot that my help doesn't matter."

I bite back a smile. "That's convenient since you don't know how to use tools." She told me that. She's a fan of those skills but doesn't have them herself.

She scowls, her hands stilling. "I can hammer a nail."

"Okay. Then what?"

She meets my eyes. "And then you hammer me against the wall."

I keep a straight face. "Hammered means drunk. You mean nail you? Screw you?"

She does some hip thrusts right up against me. "Hammer, Con."

I can't resist her. I spear my fingers through her hair and kiss her roughly. She likes that as much as I do. Her hands roam all over me and she makes these needy sounds in the back of her throat. I start backing her up toward the bed when she breaks the kiss.

"You said you'd be my fantasy man," she says softly. "Let me see you at work."

How am I supposed to hang a stupid mirror when all I can think about is driving deep inside her? Nail, screw, hammer, doesn't matter what she calls it, I need it bad.

"Please," she says.

With every ounce of willpower I have, I pull away from her. I snag a condom from the nightstand and stick it in my pocket, knowing I'm not going to be able to resist her for long.

She sits on the bed, watching my every move.

I get to work, pulling the hammer out, along with a single nail and a stud finder. There's already a wire attached to the back of the full-length mirror. I'll stick it on the wall next to the dresser. I pull the mirror out of the closet.

"Hot Builder Guy, could you take off your shirt while you work?"

Hot Builder Guy? That's a new one. I turn to face her, and she gestures for me to get started. I slowly undo the buttons of my shirt while her eyes eat me up. I'm turned on just seeing her turned on.

She holds out a hand. "Shirt, please."

I slide it off and toss it to her. She smiles and holds it up to her nose, breathing it in.

"You want to keep that?" I ask.

She drops the shirt, her cheeks flushing pink. "You always smell so good. I'll leave it with you so you can wear it more. Can I see the rear view?"

I'm beginning to feel like I'm in a strip show. It's like nothing I've ever done before with a woman, and I'm enjoying it more than I thought. And I need to erase Clint Owens from her mind. I'm her fantasy man from now on.

I give her my back and flex my muscles.

"Oh, yes," she says in a breathy voice. "Now let's see you hammer that nail."

I pick up the stud finder, turn it on, and run it along the wall.

"Ooh, a stud finder," she says. "I found one—Connor Rourke, royal stud."

A reluctant smile tugs at my lips. I grab a pencil from the

toolbox, mark the spot, grab the hammer, and drive the nail in with one stroke.

"Sexy studly builder man," she croons.

I quickly put the mirror up and turn to find her right there in front of me, naked.

She throws her arms around me. "You're officially my fantasy builder man. Now hammer me against that wall." Her mouth slams against mine.

I practically rip my clothes off all while kissing her and maneuvering her to the adjacent wall. I roll the condom on, lift her, and she wraps those long legs around me. I take her in one hard thrust, moaning in relief at the same time as she exclaims, "Yes! Like that! Hammer me."

I'm too far gone to even smile at her funny turn of phrase. I pound into her over and over, her throaty moans driving me on. Her hips lift with each stroke, taking me deeper. I'm sweating, fighting to keep control long enough…*not yet, not yet*. She goes off, her body squeezing me rhythmically, and I let go, shuddering with a powerful release as I press my lips to her neck with a long guttural groan.

She runs her fingers through my hair and, a long moment later, I lift my head to her beaming smile. I love that smile, love seeing her so happy. I kiss those smiling lips.

"Now I don't know what to call you," she says. "Stud, hot builder guy, or royal renovator."

I laugh. "Royal renovator, seriously?"

"Or my secret prince. There's so many possibilities."

"Just call me Con. Or king if you must have a nickname."

"But you're not a king, you're a prince."

"I'm the king of you, babe."

Her brows lift. "So I'm babe and you're king. That seems unbalanced."

I laugh and then I kiss her tenderly. She's just so feisty and sexy and funny. I break the kiss, stroking her hair back behind her ear, and gaze into her pale blue eyes, which seem softer now. It hits me like a hammer—I'm in love.

"What?" she asks softly.

"Nothing, babe." It's too soon and everything's still dicey with her teaching job. I lift her off me and set her down.

She grabs my arms, her legs wobbly. "If I'm going to call you king, you have to fuck me like a king. Royally. Let's make that happen soon, hmm?"

I have no idea what a royal fucking means, but it doesn't matter. I'm in. I wrap my arms around her and whisper in her ear, "You got it, babe."

~

Becca

So I'm babe. I've never been seen as the kind of woman who'd get that casual sexy nickname. Only Con sees me for the passionate woman I always wanted to be. Turns out I just never found the right guy before. The ice queen has found her king. The problem before was that my exes left me cold, not something wrong with me. It's such a relief I feel lighter, like I'm sort of floating through my day. Or maybe that's Con. He got under my skin with his gruff sweetness. I'm happier than I've been in a really long time.

I'm heading to my Thursday night office hours with a plastic container of fresh-baked chocolate chip cookies. I'm really hoping someone besides Mike shows up. Con and I decided it's best if he doesn't go to my office hours. We don't want to tempt the fates or each other in a small enclosed space. That would be so inappropriate. What can I say, the man can't resist me. And vice versa. We're like twin sparks of flame merging into an inferno. Look at me being all poetic and sexy. He brings that out in me, my royal renovator.

My phone chimes with a text just as I step into the lobby of the university building. I dig it out of my purse, hoping it's him.

Con: *Come over after. You can watch me build a kitchen table with reclaimed oak planks.*

A thrill goes through me. He speaks my lusty language—building, watching him use his muscles, reclaimed wood.

Con: *Are you turned on?*

Me: *Yes.*

Con: *Ha. There's no table. I was just dirty talking.*

I laugh out loud. He gets me. Like no one has ever gotten me before. I think I'm falling for him. My stomach dips at the thought. I never expected it would happen this way. A guy I randomly met after being stood up. A guy who's my student. Definitely not the way I normally operate.

I send a laughing emoji.

Con: *I can't wait to see you.*

My heart sings, all of me suddenly energized. Like I could dance right here in the lobby of a serious building with serious students mulling about. I smile so big my cheeks hurt. Then I realize I left him hanging and quickly text back: *Me too.*

I'm still smiling when I reach the hallway upstairs, heading toward my office. Mike's waiting for me. Damn. It's still early too.

"Hey, can I get that for you?" he asks, gesturing to the container.

"Sure, thanks." I hand it to him while I get out the key to the office from my purse, unlock it, and turn the light on. He follows me in and sets the cookies on my desk.

I walk around the desk and set my messenger bag on top and hook my purse over the chair back. "You're a bit early today." *Fifteen minutes early.*

"Finished up at work earlier than normal, so here I am. Think we'll get a crowd here with the cookies and all? Kinda like a party."

Oh my. Is this his idea of a party? "I'm not sure, but just to be safe, would you mind picking up one of those large containers of coffee from the shop down the street?" I take a seat and go for my purse. "I'll give you some cash."

He holds up a palm. "I got it, Rebecca. Anything you need."

I tuck my purse back in place. "Great, thanks."

I let out a breath I didn't realize I was holding when he leaves. It's one thing to sit through an hour of him talking my ear off, but adding on another fifteen minutes would be torture. I text Con.

Wish you were here.

Con: *You miss your king, huh? You need to be royally screwed again or hammered?*

Me: *Yes.*

Con: *You kill me, babe.*

I smile. *See ya soon, royal renovator.*

Fortunately, Mike returns along with Anita, a young brunette woman who works in pharmaceutical sales. I'm thrilled to have the company. Mike pours a coffee for himself, and I offer one to Anita. She can't stay long but wants to ask me about the paper.

I go over it with her while Mike plays with his phone.

"Thanks so much, Rebecca," Anita says. "I need to get home. Can I take a cookie for the road?"

"Of course. Take as many as you want."

She takes two and Mike helps himself to three. My mind flashes to Connor. Did he write the paper? Will it be as bad as he thinks it is? Am I going to have to explain why it's bad? Anita asked high-level questions. Connor hasn't asked any.

After she leaves, Mike says, "Finally, she's gone. Now we can have a real conversation. All she cares about is her grade. I want to dig deep into our cases. Why do we need corporate responsibility in the private sector? Isn't that what regulations are for?"

I suppress a groan. This is literally how I introduced our case study. "Well, Mike, that was the question in our last class, and the answer was an in-depth look at Axle Financial Management. They made corporate responsibility a priority, so then the question becomes what are the goals and how do we measure them, and how do we create value for the company through them. One of their first initiatives—"

He cuts me off. "Encouraging and supporting community service with their employees."

I jump right back in, trying to add to the discussion rather than recap, but he goes back again and again to my own words. It's almost like he's memorized them. I'm not sure what he's getting from this, but I find it extremely aggravating. I have the sudden urge to kick him out for wasting my time. I can't do that, though. I'm supposed to be supportive of all students, even the irritating ones.

Four cookies and a cup of coffee later—yes, that's right, I chowed down on my own cookies to stay awake—I declare our time's up. It's almost like I'm his therapist just sitting here listening. Except he's telling me my story instead of the other way around.

He stands. "Thanks, Rebecca. Another extremely enlightening meeting with you. I'm really enjoying this class."

"I'm glad to hear it. You know, I wonder if you might get more out of these meetings if you came with a question or two. It's clear you already have a grasp of the material."

He winks. "Next time."

I stand and gather my things, waiting for him to go out first.

He lingers. "Rebecca, I've been meaning to ask, are you seeing anybody?"

I freeze. Connor is supposed to be a secret. At the same time, the only reason I can think for Mike to ask is if he's interested in me. "Yes."

"Is it serious?"

I don't know. Maybe? I hope so. "Uh, I'm not sure that's any of your business."

He smiles and nods. "Fair enough. But, if it's not serious, we could grab a bite tomorrow night. Just, ya know, talk, get to know each other."

Persistent, eh? I already told him I was seeing someone.

I have to nip this in the bud. "No, thank you. I never get involved with students. That's not just my policy, it's the university's."

"Just a friendly dinner," he coaxes.

"No, thank you," I say tersely.

His eyes narrow, and I get the first real inkling of fear. "Some for the road," he says, grabbing a handful of cookies and stalking out the door.

I let out a breath. He's harmless. Everything's fine.

13

———

Becca

It's Saturday night and I'm half an hour into the two-hour faculty reception, feeling more out of place by the minute. Most of the faculty are older and showed up with their spouses. I need to fit in, make connections, and show Dean Sears that I belong here. I dearly wish Con were with me. He relaxes me. Not because of all the orgasms, though that certainly helps, it's just from his general relaxed demeanor. He's the chill I aspire to. *Sigh.* I'm not great at schmoozing. I do better with a group when there's a shared work goal.

I take a small sip of wine, making sure I don't veer into tipsy territory. I'm here on a probationary basis, and tonight feels like a test. I have to make a good impression. I wander over to a small group of my fellow professors and their spouses, listening to them talk about the new opening in the economics department. Not exactly my field. And they want a PhD with at least five years teaching experience and research credentials.

A woman with long blond hair smiles at me. "Hello, is this your first faculty reception?"

I really need to work on my game face.

I smile. "Is it that obvious?"

"You look a little lost." She offers her hand. "I'm Patricia Silver, professor of accounting."

"Nice to meet you. I'm Rebecca Edwards, adjunct professor. Right now I'm teaching a class on managing organizational change in the leadership track. I come from a management consulting background."

"Interesting," she says flatly before turning back to the group. A few seconds later, they're all laughing about someone named Howard, who fell over drunk at the previous cocktail reception celebrating the end of the school year.

I stand there for a few minutes, telling myself it's better to be on the outside of a group than alone, but I can barely stand it. I'm just not good at networking. Give me a job and I'll happily work with a team of people, but standing around making small talk with people who all seem to have known each other for years? Nails on a chalkboard. Ha! Teacher-appropriate.

I wander over to a long table with various deli and cheese platters, along with what looks like store-bought cookies. I'm picky about my cookies since I bake them myself. I take a cracker with a slice of cheese and make a new plan. Instead of inserting myself into groups and introducing myself, I'll focus on connecting with the dean. Once that happens, I'm free to go. That will be my success metric for the evening. I spot Dean Sears slapping a guy in a tweed jacket on the back, the two of them laughing uproariously. I need to wait for my moment.

I so want to pull out my phone and text Connor, but it seems bad form. No one else is on their phone. He impressed me today with his paper. I read it on the subway ride back from our class while he napped next to me. He was embarrassed for me to read it in front of him, but I just couldn't wait. His grammar wasn't perfect, but that was okay because his voice came through. Some people write very formally or with big words, trying to impress, but his case study sounded like he was just sitting next to me explaining everything, complete with sentence fragments, no commas, and various misuses of they're/there/their and you're/your. But the content, wow. A fascinating description of his family's business and its growth in what is now their second real estate development project. It's a perfect case study of change within an organization, as well as the complications of social responsibility and all the stakeholders involved in that, from government regulators, local town councils, and concerned citizens. Not to mention the difficulty of managing construction, development, and fundraising within an organization that previously only had experience with construction. He and his brothers are newly in charge after their uncle retired with no advance warning. Talk about growing pains. I'm amazed at what they've accomplished so far.

I told him we have to discuss it in class next week. At first he thought it would draw too much attention to him, but I convinced him it would be fine. We do case studies all the time, and his case is an excellent learning example. Maybe as a class we can come up with some viable solutions for his company too. That's ultimately what the class aims for.

I spot Dean Sears walking solo across the lounge, and I make my move. I'm halfway there when someone intercepts him. I stop uncertainly. Should I join this little group or wait? I'd better join them. He's only going to attract more people as he moves through the reception.

I stand next to an older bald man, who's asking the dean about golf next Saturday. I tried golf and I suck at it. I don't know why. It seems simple, but the ball just never went where I thought it would. Usually I hit it too hard, and then when I tried to compensate, it made a pathetic piddly little roll. It's a shame because it's one of those networking things that really works, particularly with men in leadership positions.

Dean Sears finally acknowledges me. "Great to see you here, Rebecca. How're you enjoying yourself?"

I nod once. "Very nice reception. And I'm really enjoying my class."

The golf buddy mutters something and walks away.

"Glad to hear it," Dean Sears says jovially. "Are you encouraging the students to join you at office hours? That's our new initiative this year as a way to connect students with the university's resources." He leans in with a smile. "One of those being our excellent faculty."

I smile back, hoping that means he's including me in the excellent assessment. "I've definitely been encouraging them. I promised home-made chocolate chip cookies. That brought two of them out."

He slaps his thigh. "Brilliant."

A middle-aged brunette woman appears at his side and smiles up at him. Dean Sears introduces us. "This is my wife, Brianna." He gestures to me. "One of our newest faculty, Rebecca Edwards. She's Joe's daughter."

I stand a little straighter at the mention of my dad and take her offered hand. "So nice to meet you."

Dean Sears smiles brightly. "Rebecca, there's an opening for a full-time position in the leadership track next semester. I encourage you to apply. I know I said we might have full-time work for you before. I was hoping to find someplace you could fit, cobbling together a few classes, but now I really do have a position to fill. I had to let one of our longtime faculty members go. You may have heard whispers about it, and I'm afraid the rumors are true."

I swallow hard. It sounds like something scandalous. "No, I haven't heard."

He presses his lips together, seeming unwilling to share the gossip.

Brianna leans in and whispers, "Professor Gage got his teaching assistant pregnant. Apparently, they were carrying on for a year in blatant violation of university policy. My husband made sure he'll never get that opportunity again."

I break out in a cold sweat. "No, of course. That's terrible."

"It would be wonderful to have someone like you take his place," Dean Sears says. "Young and enthusiastic. Provided, of course, your performance review goes well. The students' input counts for a lot." He smiles. "I'm sure it will. Your parents' reputation precedes you. Really quality educators. And your dad with New York Teacher of the Year last year."

"Yes, well deserved," I say, forcing some energy into my

voice. My parents are star teachers dedicated to their students, and then there's me, sleeping with a student. My gut does a slow roll.

Brianna puts her hand on her husband's arm, speaking quietly to him before turning back to me. "We're meeting our daughter for a late dinner tonight, so we need to go. So nice to meet you, and I hope to see you at the next reception."

"Thank you. Enjoy your dinner," I say.

They smile and take their leave, stopping to say goodbye to a few more people on their way out. I wait a safe amount of time for them to leave and head home, shaken. There's an opportunity here, waiting for me, because another professor screwed up. The similarities are not lost on me. For all I know, Professor Gage was in love with his teaching assistant. She wasn't even a student, though he would've been her boss.

I should rethink this whole thing with Connor. If he really cares about me, he'll wait for me, right?

I text Con while I wait for the subway. *Cocktail reception finished early. On my way to your place.* We made plans to see a band I like perform later tonight, but this is better because now we have time for a serious talk. I really don't want to do this, but I feel like I have to. My throat clogs with emotion, and I blink back tears. He'll understand. And, if he doesn't, then this is goodbye.

∿

Connor

The moment I open the door to Becca, I know something's wrong. She looks like she's trying not to cry, her eyes shiny, her face drawn. I pull her in and wrap my arms around her. She stands there stiffly for a moment, her arms at her sides. Then, finally, she hugs me back, holding me tight, her head buried against my chest. She had her faculty reception tonight, and I know she wanted to make a good impression.

"What happened?" I ask.

She lifts her head, her eyes watery. "The dean says there's a full-time opening in my department, which is good, but the reason is because a professor was fired for getting his teaching assistant pregnant. It's just like us." Her voice cracks.

My gut tightens as the first inkling of dread creeps through me. "No," I say firmly. "That is not like us. I don't work for you, and you're not getting pregnant."

She presses her lips tightly together. "It's the same thing in theory. You should've seen Dean Sears and his wife, the way they talked about Professor Gage like he was total scum. They said he'll never work at a university again."

Bile rises in my throat. I know exactly where this is going —she wants to end this thing between us. Everything in me rebels. I force down the awful feeling and focus on the important thing—us.

I frame her face in my hands, meeting her eyes directly. "Listen, that professor and his teaching assistant, that is not us. And you are *not* getting fired because of me. I would never let that happen. Bec, I care about you. A lot."

She swallows visibly, her voice high and reedy. "Would you wait until the end of the semester to see me?"

"No."

Her lower lip quivers. "You said you cared about me."

"I do, I swear. So much. Bec, don't ask this of me. I can't not see you, and what would be the point anyway? You'll still see me in your class. Are you going to stand up there and pretend you don't know me? Pretend you have no feeling for me at all?"

She pulls away. "That's what I've been doing so far."

"Then there's no difference if we keep seeing each other."

Her voice is soft, resigned. "The difference is I don't risk my career."

I shove a hand in my hair. I don't want to lose her, but I don't want to keep away for the next almost three months either. It'll be torture.

I take her hand and guide her over to the sofa. She sits, clutching her hands tightly together and staring at them.

I suck in air, my chest tight. I need to get the words just right, need to convince her we're worth the risk. "I don't want to lose you because of something someone else did. We didn't do anything wrong, and I promise you this is not a casual thing for me."

She meets my eyes, her lips smashed together, tears threatening.

Shit. I'm losing her. "Tonight I was going to ask you to go to my brother's engagement party in two weeks. I want to introduce you to my family. That's how much you mean to me." It's true. I was going to ask her that before my whole world tilted and threatened to throw me out on my ass.

"Really?" she asks in a choked voice. "You're not just saying that because I'm upset?"

I pull her into my lap, holding her close. "Yes, I really was going to ask you. I'm not losing you, Bec. I feel like I waited my whole life to find you."

"Okay," she says, nodding at the same time. "I'll go. I don't want to say goodbye to you either. I just felt like I had to, you know?"

I cup her soft cheek, stroking it with my thumb. "I know. But we're not wrecking us because of what other people might think." I kiss her. "Everything will be okay, I promise."

She rests her cheek against my chest and sighs. For the first time all night I feel like I can breathe again.

Nothing can come between us. I won't let it.

14

Connor

It's been two weeks since I invited Becca to Sean and Josie's engagement party, and things have been great between us. Okay, there was one dicey moment last week when we met up in the lobby after our Saturday class and Dean Sears sent us a curious look. But I convinced Becca it's okay for professors and students to talk in an academic building. Even twice. She immediately struck up another conversation with a woman from our class who had just come downstairs on her way out. Practically accosted the poor woman in her effort to look like she spent time talking to *all* her students. I calmed Becca down later that night. *Ahem.*

Anyway, tonight's the night she meets my family. We're heading to my parents' house in the Windsor Terrace neighborhood of Brooklyn.

Becca meets me in the lobby of her building, looking stunning in a sleeveless blue dress with tan heels.

I smile, taking her in appreciatively. "You look beautiful."

She frowns. "Oh no. Look at us. We match."

I'm wearing my blue button-down shirt with tan trousers. "Only a little. You're wearing a brighter blue."

"I have to change." She turns and heads for the elevator.

Good thing I got here a little early. I figured it would be

good to get to my parents' house before the party was in full swing. It's not easy for a newcomer to step into the chaos of a Rourke party, and Becca's on the shy side.

I follow her into the elevator. She punches the button and crosses her arms tightly, watching the numbers go up.

"You okay?" I ask after a long silence.

Her gaze remains riveted on the numbers. "Fine. I just need to find a good first-impression outfit. It took me a while to settle on this one, but it's okay. I'm sure I have something."

"I could go home and change."

Her head whips toward mine. "Don't be silly. I'm not sending you all the way home."

"It's three blocks away."

"It's fine, Connor. I can fix the problem."

Damn, she's wound tight. She never calls me Connor, always Con in this warm tone. I pull her arms away from her body and wrap them around my middle. She rests her cheek against my chest for a few moments, but then the elevator dings and she jerks away, rushing toward her apartment.

I follow her straight to her bedroom, which looks like a disaster area of discarded clothes and shoes. I had no idea she had this many clothes.

"I need contrasting colors from you," she says. "Maybe pants outfits are the way to go. I've got some business casual things in my armoire."

She goes to a large light wood wardrobe with double doors and flings it open. This is a separate stash of clothes from her closet. There's also a long dresser. I never paid much attention to her wardrobe before other than noticing it mostly looked corporate.

She goes through clothes at manic speed, tossing pants outfits on the bed one after the other. I'm not sure if that means she's going to try these on or they're out of the running. She pulls out a black turtleneck with black trousers and puts that back in the armoire. Shit. This could take a while. It looks like the bed stuff is to try on.

I walk around to sit on the side of the bed closest to her,

shoving her pillow out of the way. "The black outfit would look sexy on you," I say. "Put that one on."

She freezes, staring at me for a moment. "Black. I should wear my little black dress. It goes with every occasion." A few minutes later, she's wearing the sexy dress I remember from Simone's party.

"Perfect," I say, standing. Finally we can get going.

She smooths the dress as she looks down at herself. "I don't know. I think it might be too formal. More of a cocktail party dress, not an engagement party dress at someone's home."

"I'm sure there will be cocktails. At least champagne and beer."

She peels the dress off and tosses it, going back to the closet. Oh, I am liking this rear view. She's in a strapless tan lace bra with matching panties, her long legs enticing me to touch. I have to at least wait until she's picked something to wear. While she's half buried in the closet, I slip a condom from her nightstand into my pocket. No better way to deal with her nerves, I figure. So maybe we're a little late. What's worse—showing up late into chaos or being the chaos? I've got to mellow her out. It's what any good boyfriend would do.

She pulls out a green dress and a dark red dress, holding each of them up to me in question.

"Definitely the dark red," I say, liking the stretchy clingy material.

"It's burgundy." She holds it under her chin. "Boat neck, three-quarter sleeves, good for fall. But does it wash out my coloring too much?"

I don't even know what that means, but it's clear I need to take matters into my own hands. Like right away. I cross to her and take the dress, unzipping the back and kneeling at her feet for her to step into it. While she's considering complying, I stroke my palm from her ankle up the inside of her thigh to just shy of those sexy panties. Her lips part and she steps into the dress.

I rise and slowly pull the dress up over her hips, letting

my fingers trail along her skin as I do. She warms to my touch, her breath a little faster. I love watching my effect on her. I pull it all the way on, helping her into it as I touch her the whole time. It looks great. The fabric is soft, stretchy, and formfitting, which makes it easier to caress her through the dress. Her eyes go half-mast as I stroke from her long neck across her exposed collarbone over her shoulders and down her arms. I take my time caressing her breasts and then slide lower, down her stomach, coming close but never touching her sex.

"Con," she whispers.

I know I've made great progress when she calls me Con instead of Connor. *Oh, yeah, I've got the magic touch. Looks like it's full steam ahead to orgasm town.* But then she goes on.

"Is this dress really okay?"

I can't believe she's still worried about her outfit after all my caressing. What's more important here? I shift her over to the dresser to show her how fantastic she looks. There's a mirror hanging above it.

"Look. It's more than okay, it's sexy." I slowly pull the back zipper up, trailing my fingers along her spine. She shivers, and I give the nape of her neck a squeeze. "It's stretchy too. Down you go, babe." The nickname always gets a rise out of her.

"I don't think—" she starts and then quiets as I press between her shoulder blades, pushing her down over the dresser while I hitch up her dress, past her waist. I hear her sharp intake of breath as she realizes my intentions. I slide a hand between her legs, and her panties are damp. My cock surges painfully against my trousers. I get her panties off, free myself, and roll on the condom in record time. I thrust deep, and she moans.

I pull her up enough to see us in the mirror, buried deep inside her, and cup her breast with one hand. "Look how sexy you are in this dress."

"Con," she half begs.

I know exactly what she needs. I stroke her between the legs as I thrust deep over and over. She loves this. I love this.

"Con, Con, Con," she chants, and I know she's close.

"Let go," I growl in her ear, holding her firmly as I stroke faster. She makes the sexiest, neediest sounds, and then she goes off, taking me with her in a white-hot explosion of pleasure.

Unbelievably good. Every fucking time.

She's *mine*. We work on every level. I'm so glad I found her.

I kiss her cheek. "Wonderful woman." I feel her cheek curve into a smile. She called me "wonderful man" in extremely reverent tones after some of our earliest times together.

I slowly loosen my hold on her, and she sinks to the dresser limply. That relaxed her. Certainly relaxed me. I pull out and then decide I'd better get her situated. I pull those panties back up, giving her another stroke, which makes her moan, and then adjust her dress, caressing her through the fabric from her sweet ass to the nape of her neck. I give her ass a pat and she sighs. *My Becca*. Wound so tight over her outfit only to be undone by her own dress. And me.

After I get myself back in order, I find her staring at herself in the mirror. "Orgasms really are the best beauty treatment," she says in wonder. "Look how my skin glows now. There's no way I can wash out in this burgundy color."

I grin and wrap my arms around her from behind. "I'll have to become part of your beauty routine, then."

"It's an ongoing daily battle," she says, her eyes sparkling.

I nuzzle into her neck. "Is that your way of asking for daily orgasms?"

"Yes."

I meet her eyes in the mirror. "You'll have to see me daily too."

"Wouldn't be the worst thing in the world."

I nip her neck and she laughs. Warmth floods my chest in a surge of affection. I turn her to face me. "Do you know what today is?"

She nods. "The day I meet your family. Oh God, we'd

better get going. I need to freshen up." She ducks under my arm and rushes to the bathroom.

I was going to say today is our one-month anniversary. It's sappy, I know, but I'm in deep. We both are. I just hope tonight goes smoothly. I'd never tell her this, but her meeting my parents is a pretty big deal. My family is tight, and there's no way I could get serious about someone my parents didn't accept. My family is a little different on account of us being the exiled royals. Since my dad lost his other family, he made ours a priority and drummed it into us—family first. Now that we're all grown, he makes sure we get together for any and all occasions. And we all work together too. Even my dad, working in real estate, is still part of Byrne Construction, always keeping an eye out for promising properties and helping us find tenants. I mean, my parents are pretty open, friendly people, but there was that time my older brother Sean brought a woman home that my parents considered "crass." He ended it the next day. Just wasn't worth continuing when she would be a source of friction in the family. I understood.

Becca's different, though. Classy. And I got her nice and relaxed. I'm sure she'll be just fine.

~

Becca

I'm sure Con's parents will take one look at me and think *hot mess*. I walk on shaky legs down the sidewalk toward their house. I can't believe I had sex with Con before meeting them. So freaking inappropriate. The man *undoes* me. It's like my common sense just flies out the window around him. Before he showed up at my place, I spent two hours flitting like a hummingbird around my room as I attempted to get ready, nerves jangling, heart racing. I mean, I'm about to meet royalty—the king, his chosen queen, and a troop of princes! And I know how much Con's family means to him, how close they all are, working and playing together. This is a test and, if I don't pass, I wouldn't blame him for dropping me. I'd have to do the same if my parents didn't accept him, which is why I'm still terrified my parents will find out Con is my student. The people you get serious about have to fit in your life.

I try for a deep breath as we head toward the brick rowhouse where Con grew up. All my nice relaxed feeling from Con's earlier sexy efforts has vanished, though I fear I'm still sporting a giveaway orgasmic glow on my face. It's only been half an hour, but already I'm practically vibrating with tension.

I care too much about making a good impression. Con means a lot to me, and the fact that he brought me here means even more. When I even just *think* about him, my stomach flutters and I find myself smiling for no reason at all. Why couldn't I have met him after my class? Of course, then I would've first met him *in* class. Would he have approached me and asked me out? Mike did. I would've had to turn him down just like Mike. But then maybe it would've worked out after class. *Stop.* I'm way overthinking a hypothetical. The fact is, I'm in deep in a secret relationship that could very well blow up my entire life, and all I care about is that his family likes me. Like I said, no common sense around him. I should be more focused on protecting myself. But that time when I tried putting some space between us after the faculty reception, I was near tears at the thought of losing him.

I love him.

I've been afraid to say it out loud. Like it'll put too much pressure on an already delicate situation. He hasn't said it either.

Oh, God, we're here.

He gives my clammy hand a squeeze. "Don't worry. You've already met Brendan and Beast. It's just a few more people added on."

I look up at him. "You said you're the angel of the group, and I don't find you that angelic. More like a dark angel." I'm teasing, though my voice is tight with nerves. Also, I'm stalling.

He grins. "My parents made silly nicknames for us when

we were kids. They called Brendan a little devil, and he's not so bad, right?"

Brendan teases, but he seems playful about it. I'm trying to picture walking into a party with five guys like that, probably teasing Con about me. I'm not sure I can keep cool. I'll be flustered or embarrassed or defensive. I never had big brothers around teasing me before.

"Bec?"

"I guess."

He presses the bell, and my heart pounds. "My parents will just be thrilled I'm seeing someone. Ever since my sister-in-law got pregnant, they've been really gung ho on getting started on the grandparent phase of their life."

I jolt. *Is that what he's thinking for us?* I can't ask. *He's taking you to meet his parents, Becca! That means something big.* So why am I afraid one wrong move and everything will fall apart?

The door pops open to a smiling woman who must be his mom. They have the same intense blue eyes. She looks younger than I pictured, with dark brown shoulder-length hair and only a few faint lines on the fair skin of her face. I only saw her from afar in my online research. She's wearing a soft-looking V-neck white sweater with a black pencil skirt and low heels. I'm so glad I went with a dress. "Welcome! Come in, come in."

She steps back to let us in.

Con leans down to kiss his mom's cheek before making the introductions.

Mrs. Rourke beams at me, her blue eyes vibrant and sparking with energy. "Nice to meet ya, Becca. So glad ya could make it."

"Thank you for having me," I say, my tone coming out more formal than I'd like. I'm tense. I can't help it.

"What a beautiful dress," Mrs. Rourke says. "Isn't it lovely, Connor?"

"Oh, yeah, I told her that earlier," he says, giving me a sexy smile and a wink.

My cheeks flush hot. He told me; he showed me in the

mirror over the dresser; he fucked me over the dresser. I can't make eye contact with either of them.

"Everyone's in the kitchen," Mrs. Rourke says, gesturing for us to follow.

I lag behind to whisper in Con's ear, "Don't wink at me with that sexy smile, and skip the sexy voice while we're here."

He kisses my cheek. "Babe, my smile and my voice are always sexy. Can't be helped." He insists on calling me "babe," even though I never call him "king" like when we first talked about nicknames. It's weird, but "babe" has a casual possessiveness to it that gives me a jolt every time. I can't decide if I like it or not. Maybe it's because I don't have an equivalent nickname for him. Royal renovator is a mouthful. *Oh, God. Mind out of the gutter.*

"Then at least no winking, babe," I say, trying it out on him.

He widens his eyes, not even blinking. "I'll try really hard not to, babe."

I laugh. I'm fully aware I sound ridiculous insisting he not wink and use his own damn sexy voice, and he's sweet not to call me on it. He gives my hand a tug, drawing me forward through the living room. It's a beautiful space with high ceilings, oak parquet floors, and crown molding. I always notice these kinds of details. I'd say it's turn-of-the-century construction. The pocket doors separating the three rooms—living room, kitchen, and dining room—are open. The large kitchen in the center with a long island and stools is crowded with people talking over each other and laughing.

I get a flashback to the awkward faculty cocktail reception, where everyone seemed to know each other for years and I was on the outside. I try for a pleasant expression so I don't immediately come off with my frosty look that seems to put some people off.

Con goes straight to a dark-haired brother with short cropped hair and a trimmed beard, standing with his arm around a striking red-haired woman. He gives the guy a handshake, bro hug combo. "Congratulations, you two." He smiles at the woman. "Josie, welcome to the family. Hope you don't mind a little noise."

"I love it!" she exclaims. "Are you kidding me? I grew up an only child." She gestures around to the noisy group. "This is what dreams are made of!" Her voice carries so loudly that the entire room goes silent. "Oops! Was I using my last-row-of-the-theater voice again?"

Everyone laughs.

Con gestures me closer and puts his arm around my shoulders, turning me to face the group. "This is Becca. Becca, everyone."

My eyes dart from brother to brother to a pregnant woman to a few older couples, all smiling at me, looking curious.

I give them a little wave. "Hi, everyone."

"You can do better than that, Connor," a deep authoritative voice booms. "Proper introductions, please." It's the king! It has to be with that formal English and regal bearing. Con's dad, the real king of Villroy. He's in a navy blue suit, his thick dark brown hair streaked with gray, his face angular and clean shaven, his eyes a striking aquamarine. He closes the distance between us, and my heart pounds. I'm sorta fangirling over Con's dad. He gave up the crown for love. A romantic king. Does it get any better than that? At the same time, I need to make a good impression and not be awkward or tense or accidentally frosty.

"Hi," I squeak. "You must be Connor's dad."

He smiles warmly. "Daniel Rourke. Pleased to meet you, Becca…" He pauses, seeming to wait for me to fill in my last name. Will he be researching me?

"Edwards," I supply.

"Becca Edwards," he says formally. "Thank you for coming. Has anyone offered you a drink?"

"I just got here—" I start.

"Connor," he says sharply enough that *I* actually tense.

Connor turns to me and drawls, "What can I get you, Becca?" He gestures to a corner of the counter where multiple bottles of wine sit alongside various sodas.

"I'd like a chardonnay, please. Or any white wine you have is fine."

Con makes a formal bow, which I suspect is a dig at his dad's formal tone, and goes to fetch me a glass.

"So how did you and Connor meet?" Mr. Rourke asks.

Mrs. Rourke joins us. "What did I miss?"

"Your son's lack of manners," Mr. Rourke replies.

She frowns. "Come on, now, that boy is the most well-mannered of the bunch. Well, to be fair, they all know the right thing to do. The question is, do they remember what we've taught them? That's a whole 'nother thing, isn't it?"

Mr. Rourke arches a brow, clearly not happy about the breach in etiquette. "Becca was about to share how they met."

Mrs. Rourke smiles at me encouragingly, her eyes twinkling. "Do tell."

"We met at a bar," I say.

His parents exchange a glance before turning back to me, looking a little disappointed with my explanation. Crap. It sounds like a drunken hookup scene, and it kind of was, minus the drunk part. *Oh, God.* Sweat trickles down my spine, my cheeks flushing hot. They probably hoped to hear something romantic like the way they met in Paris. Con told me about it. They met at an art museum where she had an internship and he was taking a private tour. United by a love of art. Much more highbrow than meeting at a bar.

"Actually," I croak and have to clear my throat. "It was nice the way we met because my ex had just shown up, and he was rubbing it in my face that he'd gotten engaged, and, for some reason, he brought the woman for me to meet. It was extremely awkward, as you can imagine, and then Con came to my rescue and pretended to be my serious boyfriend to make it a little more even. I was alone, waiting for someone who never showed up. Con was the hero of the evening."

They both smile over at Con, who's now approaching with my wine. He's back in their good graces. He's always been in mine.

He hands me my wine, and I smile. "Thank you."

Mrs. Rourke looks from me to Con. "How long have you been seeing each other?"

I think back to when we first met, about to do a quick calculation, but Con replies first.

"A month," he says, kissing my temple.

My heart squeezes, my knees weak. His tender kiss combined with the fact that he actually kept track of how long we've been together just undoes me. I lean against his side, smiling, and he puts an arm around me, giving me a sideways hug.

"Very nice," Mrs. Rourke says. "I hope to see more of you around here, Becca."

"Thank you," I say, feeling so warm and relaxed now. I think I passed the test, and there's no place I feel more comfortable than pressed against Con's side.

"You should introduce Becca to everyone," Mr. Rourke says. "And I mean individually, so she actually knows everyone's names."

I smile even wider. *I'm in!*

Con nods once at his dad and lifts a hand. "Hey, everyone, look this way and raise your hand when I call your name. Becca needs a formal introduction."

Mr. Rourke shakes his head sadly. Mrs. Rourke hides a smile.

Con goes on. "Dylan."

"Present," his brother replies.

Everyone laughs. I smile and wave at him. I remember him from his wedding pictures online.

Dylan holds up his wife's hand. "This is my beautiful pregnant wife, Ariana."

"My daughter," a middle-aged woman pipes up. "Hi, I'm Mrs. Bianchi, a friend of Con's mom, and now we're family since our kids married. Where're ya from, Becca?"

"Queens."

"Queens! A hometown girl, eh?" she says, looking pleased. "Not the same as Brooklyn, but close." She smiles over at Mrs. Rourke.

"Back to the introductions," Con says, pointing out another brother. "Jack and Riley."

"So now we're like one name?" Jack asks. "Geez, as soon as you get engaged, you become Rack."

Riley grins. "More like Jiley."

"Jiley Wourke," they say in unison and crack up.

Connor leans down to my ear. "It's Jack Rourke and Riley Walsh mashed together. They're so disgustingly in love." He straightens, his eyes warm on mine, and then he winks.

I love this man. I love his warmth, his casual acceptance of mushy-in-love couples, his easy way with me, the way he just gets me. He takes my breath away. He really is a catch. My elation over finally finding the man I want to settle down with is tempered by a stab of fear. I can't let outside circumstances ruin what we have. *Don't think about that right now.*

Con's expression changes, becoming more serious. "You okay, babe?"

I nod, my throat clogged with emotion. I'm his babe and, yes, I do like it. I've never been anyone's babe before. It's just like when he carried me after I fell that first night we met. He sees me for the person I really am on the inside, warm with a lot of love to give, touchable, passionate. Not an ice queen.

"You know me," a deep voice says.

I turn to Brendan now standing in front of me. "Of course, Brendan. You put in a good word for Con here the night we met."

"That's right." He turns to Con and smacks his shoulder. "Where's my thank you, bro?"

"Bite me," Con says. "Stay in your corner."

Brendan shakes his head, smiling. "See what I hafta put up with? I'll let ya deal with him."

Beast approaches and offers his hand, enveloping my much smaller hand in a firm handshake. "Glad to see ya again."

"Ooh, me, me!" the red-haired Josie says, raising her hand. I remember her from when we first came in. "Do me next. I'm the reason we're all here tonight. If it wasn't for me, Sean here wouldn't be engaged. He'd be wandering the earth, still searching for his soul mate."

Sean gives her a tender smile. "Aww, Josie."

Con points them out. "Josie is Sean's fiancée, our new sister—"

"Aww, you called me sister!" Josie exclaims, rushing over to hug Con and kiss his cheek. "You're just as sweet as your brother."

Con smiles, looking a little embarrassed. He turns to me. "If you couldn't tell, Josie is an actress."

"What's that supposed to mean?" Josie asks, parking a hand on her hip and tossing her long red hair. "How could she tell?"

Sean joins us. "Your voice that reaches the entire neighborhood, your bubbly personality, the expressive dramatic way you speak."

"Well, damn," she says, batting her eyes innocently. "I thought I was so subtle."

I stifle a laugh. "Great to meet you both."

"Josie just wrapped her first movie," Sean says proudly. "You get to say you knew her when. She's gonna be a huge star."

"Sean!" Josie exclaims, rubbing his chest and smiling up at him. "Stop embarrassing me. It was a supporting role."

"You can tell she hates it, right?" Sean teases.

"Few more people," Con announces, pointing out some older couples. They all smile at me.

I wave. "Hello, everyone."

Con turns to his dad. "Now can we go back to the party, sir?"

His dad grunts, and the party goes back to full swing, everyone talking and laughing again. Con's mom starts taking food out of the refrigerator, and I go over to offer my help.

"I'd love that, Becca," she says warmly. "Here, take the chopped veggies. My boys will probably skip over them, but the rest of us can enjoy. So, what do you do for a living?"

"I teach a business class at NYU on managing organizational change, and work at a coffee shop, too, just part time for the health insurance. I'm hoping to be full-time teaching next semester."

"Con's taking a business class at NYU." Her brows draw together. "Actually, that sounds like the class, something about managing change. I remember I thought it was perfect for our family business." She turns and calls to Con, who's talking to his uncle, "Con, what was the name of that class you're taking?"

My heartbeat roars in my ears, my cheeks flushing hot. Con catches my eye before saying to his mom, "Managing organizational change."

"Yes, that's what—" She points at me and stops herself. "Is she your teacher? Is that how you really met?"

"What's this, now?" Brendan asks with a laugh. "Con, are you hot for teacher?"

Someone whoops in a low tone, and then the entire room goes quiet, everyone staring at me. Nausea rises in my throat.

Mr. and Mrs. Rourke exchange a concerned look. I can't take it. All of my worries and fears and shame are out for everyone to judge.

I turn to go, and suddenly Con is there, his hand clamped around my wrist. "It's not a big deal," he says to the room. "I'm auditing the class, no grade for me. Becca's a great teacher."

"How great is she?" Brendan teases.

I yank free of Con's grip and rush toward the front door, mortified. I can never show my face here again.

15

———

Connor

"Becca!" She's walking toward the subway. She can't just leave like this. It's worse than if she dealt with the fallout. It makes it look like what we're doing is wrong.

I go after her. "Wait!"

"No. Just let me go." I can hear the tears in her voice.

I catch up with her a few moments later, grabbing her around the middle from behind. She goes stiff as a board. I lean down to her ear. "It's fine. Brendan's teasing. It's not that bad."

"It is bad," she says in a strangled voice. "Your parents must think I'm a horrible person."

"My mom was surprised because you told her we met at a bar, and then it turns out you're my teacher. It's a strange situation the way things went for us, but if you come back and we explain it, I promise you it'll be fine."

"No, it won't. They'll judge me."

I turn her to face me and tip her chin up. "They won't."

"They'll think I took advantage of their son," she whispers, blinking back tears.

"They know that no one could take advantage of me. I wouldn't let them. That's how I was raised. I stand up for myself and everyone else I love." I cup her cheek. "Come back. Let me stand up for you."

She sucks in air, her eyes widening.

"I love you, Becca."

She bursts into tears.

I pull her close, stroking her hair. "Not exactly the response I was hoping for, babe."

She hugs me tight. "I love you too."

"I know, but it's damn nice to hear."

She laughs, and I let out a long breath of relief.

Tonight went great. Well, after I explained the situation and sang Becca's praises, saying how smart and business savvy she is, and then she jumped in to tell everyone how smart and business savvy I am, and it was basically a big lovefest with lots of witnesses. Sure, I took a lot of ribbing from my brothers, but they kept Becca out of it after I threatened payback. They know it takes a lot to piss me off, but once there, I don't mess around.

She stuck to my mom like glue for the rest of the night, helping her set out food, serve up drinks, and even slicing the huge Happy Engagement sheet cake and giving it out to everyone. I think Becca wanted to be part of things, but felt more comfortable doing something. I get that. I like to take action more than sit back watching others do stuff. She hit it off with Riley too. At one point, they had a killer Ping-Pong match going in the basement rec room. Not too surprising that they connected. Riley's also a corporate type, an accountant at a prestigious firm, as well as being on the more reserved side.

Now we're all gathered in the kitchen again, finishing up our cake.

My dad holds up his champagne glass and clinks the side of it with his fork for attention.

"Another toast," Brendan groans. "We get it. Sean and

Josie are special and we love them so much. Can we move it along?"

Dad shoots him a warning look before taking us all in. "I have an announcement."

The room goes entirely silent, tension thick in the air. I exchange a nervous look with Dylan and do a quick check-in with Jack, Sean, Brendan, and Beast. No one has a clue what this is about. Last time we had a big announcement at a family party, we had the shock of my uncle retiring and leaving the construction company to me and my brothers. Complete surprise. None of us prepared for it in the least. Now what?

Mom smiles. "Your dad's very excited about this. Go on, honey."

Dad takes a deep breath. "We're invited to Christmas on Villroy."

Josie lets out a whoop, and Riley lets out her own version, saying, "Wow, so exciting!" They've never been to the palace.

I'm not so excited. Neither are my brothers from the look of them and their complete nonreaction. This could get dicey. My parents will want us all to be together for Christmas. My brothers and I have been to Villroy twice, once for our cousin Adrian's wedding, which was excruciatingly uncomfortable since it was the first time our family had returned to Villroy since the exile, and then for Dylan's wedding, which was heavily covered by the press. Both formal occasions, both kinda stressful. We had to be on our best behavior, best manners, best dress. The riffraff sons of the exiled king could *not* embarrass him. My dad has high standards from his royal upbringing. It's not exactly *fun* to put it mildly, though we did have a good time playing poker with our cousins late at night.

Becca squeezes my hand, her eyes lit up with excitement. I almost forgot, she's into the royal thing.

"No reaction?" Dad asks. "I thought you'd be more excited. It's no cost to us. The royal jet will take us there, and we can all stay at the palace."

Becca fidgets by my side, fighting a smile. The women in the room are all smiling, looking very pleased about everything. It occurs to me Becca would really like to go, and I'd like that too, spending Christmas together.

Dad goes on. "There will be a themed Christmas ball a few days before Christmas."

My brothers and I groan. *A ball? What is this, the eighteen hundreds?*

Mom shoots us all a quelling look that says *knock it off*. We get quiet.

Dad huffs. "The theme is Regency England because your cousin's wife writes stories set in that time frame. It's all in the email. I'll forward it to you. There's some recommended reading, Jane Austen especially…" He trails off at the collective groan of the men in the family.

"Jane Austen is da bomb," Josie quips. Everyone laughs.

"Yes," Dad says. "Thank you, Josie." He takes in us guys. "Your mother and I are going, and I'd like you all to be there too." He cracks a smile, his eyes going soft. "Mila's been asking for Pop-Pop." Mila is the king's two-year-old daughter, and my dad is her Pop-Pop. He stepped into the grandfather role since both of Mila's grandfathers passed away. (He's technically her great-uncle.) It was how the ruling king and queen brought my dad back into the kingdom, and he took to it with his whole heart. He loves that little girl.

Dad goes on in a voice choked with emotion. "This is the first Christmas she has an inkling what's going on. I want to be part of it."

My brothers and I glance at each other. Dad and Mila together for Christmas. We know we can't say no. We all want to see him happy, to have his original family and still have us too.

"I'll be there," I say.

Becca's head snaps up, meeting my eyes for a brief moment of obvious excitement before looking away. She's definitely hoping to go with me. Pure joy lights me up inside at the thought.

"Thank you, Connor," Dad says. "Anyone else?"

"We're out," Dylan says. "It's two weeks from Ariana's due date, and she can't fly then."

Brendan coughs out, "Lucky."

Dylan grins.

"Really sorry we have to miss," Ariana says, rubbing her stomach. She must be about seven months along. "Another year."

"We'll have you two at our place for Christmas!" Mrs. Bianchi exclaims. That's Ariana's mom. She's a bit over-bearing though well-meaning.

Dylan's smile falters before he says smoothly, "We'd love to. Thank you, Mrs. Bianchi."

She beams at him and nods at Mrs. Rourke. They approve of his manners. *What a kiss-up.*

"There's a spa, ladies," Mom says in a coaxing voice. "We could have a girls' day."

"I'm there, Mrs. Rourke," Josie says.

"Me too," Riley says.

Sean and Jack grumble their agreement now that their women roped them into it.

Beast lifts a hand and nods. He's in.

Dad turns to Brendan, the holdout.

Brendan gives him a pained look. "Do I really have to go to a Regency whatever ball and read Jane Austen?"

"Yes," we all yell back at him.

He throws his hands up. "Fine. I'm not spending Christmas alone. You forced my hand. But no Jane Austen. I've seen those movies advertised on TV with their bonnets and the guys are wearing weird short pants and tights."

Ariana pipes up. "Read some of Alice's Regency romance, Bren." Alice is my cousin's wife. "Might open your eyes to a little bit more than history." She lifts her brows, grinning. I've heard Alice's stories don't leave out the good parts. Not that I'm going to read a girly love story.

"Ha! Romance," Brendan says, the tips of his ears red. "Don't need a book for that."

We all rib him mercilessly because he's basically a Nean-derthal when it comes to women. He thinks he's got game, but he's got nothing to back it up. No substance, all surface, all about the meaningless hookup. Jack used to be the same way, but he's changed since Riley barreled into his life.

"The Rourkes are going back to Villroy!" my uncle yells.

"Huzzah!" my dad cheers, outing himself as the non-New Yorker he is. I don't care how long he's lived in Brooklyn, he's still a Villroy king at heart.

Josie and Riley talk excitedly with my mom about the trip. My brothers talk amongst themselves, looking a lot less excited.

I turn to Becca and whisper in her ear, "Do you want to go to Villroy for Christmas?"

She smiles, and I kiss that smiling cheek. "Yes."

She gazes into my eyes and in that moment I know. I can finally relax. It's smooth sailing from here on out.

She leans on my shoulder with one hand and says softly by my ear, "By then, I'll know if they're going to keep me on as a professor, and you and I should be out of questionable territory. It'll be so nice to be in the clear."

"That's the plan." A dark thought slowly dawns. If they don't keep her on as professor, will she blame me? No, she wouldn't do that. I think. It's hard to tell because she gets really worked up about the ethics of the situation we're in.

I can't let myself dwell on that. We're keeping everything quiet, and Becca is great at her job. We'll keep on doing what we're doing, and everything will be fine. It has to be.

16

———

I walk with a bounce in my step to my meeting with Dean Sears. Class ends in two weeks, and I think this is my performance review where I find out if they're going to give me that full-time position. I'm feeling pretty good about it. Last week, just before Thanksgiving break, they sent out surveys for the students to rate their teachers. I'm sure they'll be good. Class has been going exceptionally well. There's lots of great discussion going on, and I've reached a comfort level and trust in Con that means I can really enjoy his participation. We've gone into his family business's case study in great depth, and it's made for a fantastic learning experience for everyone. And things with Con couldn't be better. He spent Thanksgiving with my family, and I'm joining him in Villroy for Christmas. To think I was so worried about being involved with him when it's the best thing that's ever happened to me. Just thinking about him makes me smile.

My meeting is an hour before my Thursday night office hours, which are rarely attended. I really tried, but after I turned Mike down for dinner, he stopped showing up, and I only occasionally see someone with a question about a paper. I'll have to confer with other professors to see if there's anything further I can do to improve that for my next class.

I'd like to teach this one again in the spring, and hopefully I'll have a full-time load of classes too.

I step into the meeting room, a large space with a wall of windows, one long conference table, and chairs. Two people sit on one side of the table—Dean Sears and the human resources director, Cheryl Boggs. My stomach drops like a rock. Cheryl is probably in her forties with thin blond hair and a round face that usually looks cheerful, but today she looks serious. So does Dean Sears.

Don't panic. Maybe they bring in HR for hiring decisions. You did interview with her before. Maybe she's here to go over the paperwork.

My gut churns, unconvinced. Something is very wrong. I take a seat. "Hi, how're you?"

"Just fine, Rebecca," Cheryl says gently.

Dean Sears shuffles some papers in front of him. "How're things going with class, Ms. Edwards?" He lifts his head, his expression hard to read.

I try for a confident tone. "It's going really well. We've had a lot of great class discussion around our case studies, good participation, too. I feel like we're all learning a lot from each other."

"Uh-huh," Dean Sears says.

"Anything else you'd like to tell us?" Cheryl asks.

My mind whirls. Do they know I'm involved with Con? I can't out myself. Maybe it's something else.

I lift my shoulders in a small shrug. "I'm still bringing home-made cookies to office hours, though I admit attendance has dwindled. It's one of the things I was going to work on for next semester. Right now everyone's very focused on the final paper, and they seem to have a handle on it."

They exchange a look. Dean Sears gestures for Cheryl to speak.

I turn to her, heart in my throat.

"Rebecca, a student has filed a complaint against you. They say it was obvious you were involved with a student in your class."

I immediately think of Mike ratting me out. I told him I was seeing someone and maybe he realized it was Con. "Well, a student did ask me out, Mike Ahern, and I declined his invitation. It's possible he's lashing out." It's a stretch because I knew all along the optics looked very bad on the Connor front.

"This complaint was filed by a woman in your class," Dean Sears says, putting his glasses on and referring to a paper in front of him. I lean forward, but I can't read it from across the table. "She says—" he clears his throat "—the steamy looks between you and this male student made her uncomfortable. She felt triggered because as an undergrad she had a professor take an interest in her."

My gut knots. I never wanted to make anyone feel bad because of my actions. "No one said anything to me," I force out over the lump in my throat.

"She didn't feel comfortable telling you directly," Cheryl says. "She hoped we would deal with it."

Oh God. My face is hot with shame, nausea rising in my throat. "I never meant for this to happen, but you have to believe me, this isn't a predatory situation. It's consensual. I met him before class began."

Dean Sears gives me a skeptical look. "The student you were involved with is named here, Ms. Edwards. I saw you with him in close conversation at the beginning of the semester. You told me you'd just met."

Crap. I did say that, and I insisted I was single, which can only mean I started seeing Con after that, while he was a student in my class. This looks so damning. "I, uh…"

Dean Sears lowers his glasses down his nose to meet my eyes directly. "I saw you together again a few weeks later, looking very comfortable together. What am I supposed to think?"

"I know it looks bad." My voice cracks. "The first time you saw us, I panicked and lied. We actually had met before and we were together. I—"

"And how do I know you're not lying to me now?" he demands.

I open my mouth and shut it again. The seeds of doubt have been planted by my own doing. Bile rises in my throat.

Cheryl chimes in. "Rebecca, do you admit to being involved with a student?"

"Yes, but we were involved before class began, I swear. I didn't know he was going to be my student."

Cheryl writes something in her notes. Dean Sears shakes his head, regarding me with a disappointed look. He thinks I'm backpedaling to cover it all up. The evidence is right in front of him from the complaint against me.

Cheryl cocks her head. "Did you ever discuss with him ahead of time about signing up for your class?"

She's trying to give me the benefit of the doubt. Assuming what I said is true—that we were already in a relationship— we would've talked about my class.

My shoulders droop, a dull ache in my chest. "No." *How can I explain that we had a wild one-night stand the day before class and never really talked?*

Dean Sears looks resigned. Cheryl wears an almost angelically gentle expression. She's probably trained for this kind of sensitive situation.

"He's auditing the class," I say desperately. "Technically, not even a real student."

"But he's been attending with the other students, correct?" Cheryl asks.

I nod. Obviously they know Con's been in class or we wouldn't be having this discussion.

"Could I just talk to her?" I ask. "The student who filed a complaint? I'll apologize and explain the situation. I'm sure if we could just talk, this would clear right up."

"I can't share her identifying information," Cheryl says. "We put students first here. They need to feel safe and supported."

"They were," I say. "They are. This is all just a misunderstanding."

Cheryl nods, her tone soothing. "Be that as it may, it still made for an uncomfortable environment for the other students. We always send out a survey for feedback before

the final exam or project, and your reviews were overwhelm-
ingly poor. Some were downright scathing."

I go cold, staring at her in shock. "They were?"

"Yes."

My voice comes out in a whisper. "I really thought things
were going well." I can't believe everyone hated me as a
teacher. "We had some good discussions. It seemed they were
learning from the questions they asked."

Dean Sears pushes his glasses in place, scanning a paper
in front of him. "They said almost universally that you were
inattentive, distracted, and spent too much time on your
favorite student."

"I didn't have a favorite." *Did I?* I really did think
Connor's case study was a good learning tool.

Dean Sears runs his finger down the paper. "Says here you
spent three weeks discussing a development project in detail
as though you were a consultant to your boyfriend's
company."

"I'm not. I just thought it was an interesting case study
and we could all learn from it." I look from Dean Sears to
Cheryl, pleading with them to understand.

Dean Sears exhales sharply. "Perhaps your involvement
led to your inattention to other students in class and caused
you to fixate on him."

I break out in a cold sweat. Crap. I never should've let this
thing happen with Con. I had my doubts from the beginning.
Yes, he made me happy, but at what price?

"I swear I wasn't inattentive to the other students," I say
in a last-ditch effort to save my job.

Dean Sears takes off his glasses and folds his hands in
front of him on the table. "I'm sorry, Rebecca, but it's not
going to work out. You won't be staying on here at the
university."

My eyes are hot. I'm so filled with shame and regret I can
only stare blankly at him, out of words, out of ways to defend
myself.

"Can I at least finish out the semester?" I ask. "There's
only three more classes and I've prepared material."

Dean Sears stares at me for a long moment. "If you feel you can do so within the proper bounds of the rules of this university."

I nod, my throat too tight to speak.

"Rebecca," Cheryl says gently.

I blink and turn to her, tears blurring my vision.

Her eyes are full of gentle understanding. "Unfortunately, we do have to disclose that there was a complaint lodged against you if a reference calls us in the future."

My gut churns as the full impact of this horrendous mistake hits me—I'll never work in academia again. My entire career finished after one class. I'd thought Con and I handled it so well, but it's just as I feared. All the risk was on me all along.

"Do you understand everything we've discussed here today?" Cheryl asks with a note of finality. There's nothing more to say. I'm finished.

I stand on wobbly legs. "Yes, I understand. Dean Sears, please don't share this with my father. I want him to hear it from me."

Dean Sears gives me a long look. "If he asks me why I let you go, I'm not going to lie."

I swallow hard, nod, and walk on stiff legs out the door.

I make it all the way to my office upstairs before I burst into tears. I feel horrible that I caused another student pain by my actions. If I'd known, I would've explained. I never, ever wanted to cause anyone pain. And now I have to deal with the consequences of my actions. My parents would be so ashamed if they knew. They were so proud I wanted to be teachers after their example. I can't tell them yet. I just can't.

I rest my forehead on my desk. All my plans blew up in my face. I knew seeing Con was a bad idea, but I caved. Now I'm lost without a path.

I'm through.

It's Friday night, and Connor is on his way over. I've been too depressed to get off the sofa. I'm not looking forward to this conversation. I haven't told him about the meeting yesterday, too upset to talk about it. I don't think he'll understand the terrible pain and humiliation losing my job is. And I still have to show my face in class tomorrow. It'll be difficult, but I want to see it through and, if possible, move forward in the most positive teaching environment possible. It kills me that a student is hurting because of something I did. I want a chance to make it better. My eyes sting with tears again, and I scrub them away. I'm so tired of crying. I had to skip my office hours after that horrible meeting, and I now realize the reason they were so poorly attended was because no student wanted to work with me. I'm officially a failure as a teacher. It's especially shameful in light of how seriously my parents take the teaching profession. My dad is the freaking New York Teacher of the Year.

The intercom buzzes, and I drag myself over to the door to answer it.

His familiar deep voice comes through. "Hey, babe, it's me."

I slap a hand over my mouth to cover my sob. He'll take my side, but my side is wrong because he's in it. I have to be strong and finally do the right thing. I hit the buzzer to let him into the building.

A few minutes later, I let him into my apartment. He takes one look at me and rushes forward, pulling me into his arms. "Bec, what's wrong? You're still in your pajamas and you look like you've been crying." I'm wearing an oversized T-shirt and my gray cotton jogging pants. I've basically been on a crying jag for the past twenty-four hours.

I lean against him for a long moment, my frazzled nerves temporarily soothed. Then I remember myself and pull away. "We need to talk."

"Uh-oh."

"Yeah." I go to my sofa, tucking a leg under me.

He joins me.

I smooth my messy hair out of my face. "I didn't leave the apartment today. In fact, I didn't leave the sofa."

"Okay," he says slowly. "Why not?"

I grip my hands tightly together and stare at them. "I was too ashamed."

He takes my hand in his and cups my cheek with his other hand, turning me to face him. "Bec, I can't imagine *you* did anything that bad. You're one of the best people I know."

I shake my head. "No, I'm not."

"What happened?"

I tell him the whole horrible story in between bursts of tears. I'm not even sure I'm making sense. Talking about what happened in that meeting brings fresh pain.

"Shit." He rubs the back of his neck. "Bec, I never wanted this on you. I accept full responsibility for pushing to keep seeing each other. I just couldn't not be with you. I love you, you know that."

I bite my trembling lip, nodding and desperately holding back tears.

He scoots closer, rubbing my back. "I'm so sorry. Let me talk to the dean. I'll fix it."

"No!"

"Bec."

"No, it's too late and that'll just make it worse." I grab a tissue from the end table and wipe my eyes before blowing my nose and crumpling the tissue in my fist.

"I have to do something. It's my fault."

I glance at his pained expression. "No. It's not all on you. I made my own choices, even as conflicted as I was. With good reason, right?" I laugh mirthlessly. "I don't know what to do now—about you, about work, about anything."

"Whoa, what do you mean you don't know what to do about me? You said you didn't blame me."

I sit there for a long moment, lost in the turmoil of all my careful plans blowing up in my face. I'm overheated, agitated, my mind careening from regret to shame, all of it directed at my poor choice. I knew better. I should've listened to my gut.

I take a deep breath. "I think we should stop seeing each other."

His jaw clenches. "Pushing me away isn't going to bring your job back."

"I don't have a job because of us," I say quietly.

"No, it's because someone has their own issue and they made it yours."

I throw my hands up. "It's a legitimate complaint, Connor. I created a hostile environment for my students."

He scoffs. "Ridiculous."

"It's not ridiculous. If it was, this whole thing wouldn't have blown up in my face."

"Bec, listen, I'll talk to the dean and explain everything."

I leap off the sofa. "There's nothing to explain! There's just the facts, and they're all lined up against me." I cross my arms, hugging myself. "Please go. I need to figure some things out."

He stands. "We can figure things out together."

I look toward the door. "I need some space. Can you please respect that?"

I hear his sharp exhale and then he leaves, giving me the space I asked for. I close my eyes and lift my head to the ceiling, trying to hold the tears back. A losing battle.

Finally, I decide to change and go for a run in Prospect Park, hoping it'll clear my head.

The run just wears me out even more. Now I'm physically and emotionally spent. My phone rings on my cooldown walk. I check the screen. Simone. I called her earlier but got her voicemail. She was probably in a recording session, working on her next album.

"Becca, I just got your message. Honey, are you okay?"

I take a seat on a nearby bench. "No. It's horrible. My parents would be so ashamed. I'm so ashamed."

"Just because you lost your job?"

"No, it was more than that." My voice cracks, and I take a deep breath before spilling my guts with all the damning details.

"That's bullshit," she says.

"No, it's not. My students had a legitimate complaint.

Maybe I was unintentionally playing favorites. I just really thought his case study was a good learning experience."

"They can't fire you for this," she says hotly.

"I wasn't fired. They just didn't ask me back. The worst part is, there was a formal complaint against me that they have to disclose to future employers, so I'm basically finished in academia."

"Oh, Bec. I'm so sorry. I know you really wanted this new career to work out for you."

I stare at the ground. "What's the point of planning when it just blows up in my face? I'm an idiot for thinking I could have it both ways, keep my job and my—" I choke. "I don't think it's going to work out with Con."

"I'm sorry."

I sniffle. "Thanks."

"I know everything is shit right now, but I could still really use you on my team. Come out to LA. We'll talk more and I'll introduce you around. We'll see how you feel after that. Wouldn't you like a little getaway?"

"Yeah, I would actually." I did say I'd consider being her business manager after I finished my semester. Now I'm really finished. I close my eyes and let out a long breath.

"Okay. I know you have class on Saturday. How's Sunday? I'll have my assistant arrange everything. We'll have you back in time for your next class. Can you get time off your other job?"

"Yeah, I think so."

"Awesome. I'm psyched. You'll love it out here, sunshine all the time."

I try to put some enthusiasm in my voice, though I feel numb. "Okay. Looking forward to seeing you."

17

———

Bec is off her game in class today. I gave her some space, hoping she'd get her bearings, and it's been brutal wondering if this is the end of us. I've never seen her like this before. She keeps stopping and starting the lecture, her gaze anxiously studying the women in class. She really wants to talk to whoever complained about her, and apologize. I don't think she did anything wrong, and I'm not just saying that because I'm the one she's seeing. Bec has been nothing but professional in class. If she occasionally looks at me with real affection in her eyes, that's just normal. She's not a robot. You can't just turn off your feelings. But there's been nothing overt. I never touch her, flirt with her, or even speak directly to her unless called upon. I've been very careful, as I promised her from the beginning.

Class limps along, and it's painful to watch. It was Becca's enthusiasm that kept things going, and she's lost that.

Once class lets out, I leave with the others and wait for her outside the building. We need to talk. She appears a few moments later, pulling the hood up of her long white down coat, huddled against the cold.

I step into her path. "Hey, Bec."

She jumps. "Con, we can't be seen together."

"It's a little late for that, isn't it?"

She blinks rapidly, her eyes tearing. "I just want to get home. I need to do laundry and pack." She walks at a brisk pace to the subway and I keep up.

"Why're you packing? Where're you going?"

"LA. I'm going to visit Simone. She might have a job I'm right for, working for her."

My gut tightens. "You're moving to LA for a new job?"

"I don't know, Connor. It's a possibility, and I need to get away. She's been asking me to be her business manager for a while now, she really needs me, and now that I'm unemployed, I need to consider it."

"Did you consider us?"

"What about us?"

I stop her, putting a hand on her arm. "I'm rooted here with my family business, you know that. So you make these plans without even talking to me about it?"

She shoves her hood off. "What would you say?"

"I'd say don't go."

"See? I need to consider what's best for me. I didn't do that before, and now my whole life blew up."

My chest aches. "You do blame me."

She shakes her head. "I know it was both of us, but, Con, I need space to figure things out. It's too easy for me to forget about what *I* want when we're together."

She turns from me, walking away maybe forever, and desperation rears its ugly head.

"So you just run away from your problems and let Simone take care of you?" I bark.

She turns back. "It's a real job. And I've got nothing to lose."

"So I'm nothing to you."

She crosses her arms. "I didn't say that."

I close the distance. "It feels like we both lose. Fight for us."

"Please." She backs away, her face crumpling. "Just give me the space I asked for." She hurries off, and I let her go.

I stand there, watching her retreating back. I'm losing her.

It's all falling apart before my eyes, and I have no idea how to fix it.

Becca

I'm back after a week in LA. I feel calmer now about my life implosion. Nothing like being with your best friend for comfort and support. I still have a lot to figure out, but Simone gave me a killer pep talk, and I'm going to hold my head high and finish this class to the best of my abilities.

I arrive early to class on Saturday morning and take my place at the lectern. There's only two classes left. Today I'm going to cover addressing new corporate priorities through restructuring. The last class is when the final paper is due, and each student will present what they wrote about to the class. Basically, today is my last day of instruction, and I'm going to make it the best I possibly can.

I get my notes out as my students arrive. It still hurts that my performance reviews were so poor, but as Simone says, what other people think of me is not my concern. I'm sure that works better when you're a celebrity. Deep down, I'm still gutted that my first foray into what I thought was my destiny has been such a spectacular failure. I can't put all the blame at Connor's feet. I made my choice. And maybe I was unintentionally distracted by his presence; maybe I did send him longing looks without realizing it. The fact is there were two of us involved in this relationship. After class, I'm going to ask him to come back to my place. We have so much to talk about.

I start off the lecture strong, telling myself my students are actually looking forward to learning from me. I'm halfway through discussing a company I consulted with previously on their restructuring to address sustainability goals when I realize no one is taking notes. In fact, the class is eerily quiet. Maybe I didn't leave enough room for participation.

I take them in with what I hope is an encouraging expression. "Does anyone have an example of new corporate goals and how they were implemented? Bonus if it involved new job titles and new lines of direct reporting." That's a little joke because I'm asking them to give me the example I just gave them.

No one even looks up.

I take a deep breath. "Okay, so back to Regenerix's example. A new department of sustainability was created with direct report to the president of the company to make sure all corporate goals were aligned with sustainability goals." I glance up at the murmur of voices. Mike, sitting right up front, is talking to his neighbor in a low voice. Several people are on their phones.

I clear my throat. "If I could please have your attention, I know it's early on a Saturday, but this is the second to last class, and I'm really hoping you'll come away with some useful information."

Nothing. People are tuning me out. Do they hate me as a teacher that much?

"Mike, please save your private conversation for later," I say.

His eyes narrow into slits. "Yes, ma'am."

"No need to call me ma'am," I say lightly. "That sounds like my mother." I laugh a little. The class stares back at me blankly, a few with dark expressions.

I soldier on, staring at my notes. "Well, we're all here for a reason so let's get back to—"

"I'd like to say something," a familiar deep voice calls out.

My head jerks up. *Oh no.* Connor is standing looking like he's about to make a big announcement.

I shake my head at him.

He lifts a palm with a small nod of acknowledgment to me but goes on anyway. "I just want to clear the air. There's been some talk about Rebecca and her involvement with me. I want everyone to know that we were involved before class even started, so there was no kind of abuse of power or anything inappropriate between us. It was—is, simply a relationship between two consenting adults. And I'm auditing this class—no grade for me—so the fact that we're involved really has no impact on any other student."

My mouth gapes in shock; my eyes and cheeks hot. I swallow a few times, speechless.

He takes his seat. The class is utterly silent.

I look from face to face, everyone looks uncomfortable. A few women shift in their seats and look down at their laptops. I'm so humiliated. How can I go on?

"Fifteen-minute break," I say and bolt from the room.

I don't want to see anyone. I can't chance the ladies' room. I go upstairs, hoping for privacy in my office, but a custodian is cleaning it. I find an empty meeting room, shut the door behind me, and stare out the window. How could he do this to me? On what planet is addressing the class with a big announcement about our personal life ever appropriate? And to think I was finally ready to move past all this.

The door opens. "Bec?"

He followed me. Of course he did. He just does what he wants no matter how it looks to other people. I hear the door shut quietly behind him.

I turn to face him, waiting for him to get close enough that I can speak softly and only he can hear me. "You crossed the line. Y-you—" My voice shakes with anger and I have to take a calming breath. "You made the issue public, which made it worse. And you didn't discuss it with me ahead of time!" My voice gets loud at the end there, but I can't help it.

He scowls. "You went away and didn't discuss your plans with me ahead of time either. How's it feel?"

I blink a few times, speechless. No apology, no remorse, just throwing that in my face. I can't believe this is the man I risked my career over. Damn him.

"Shitty, Con. It feels shitty. And I don't like a relationship that keeps score. Don't come back to class. Don't...just don't do anything. I can't see you anymore."

His jaw clenches, his eyes narrowing. I pissed him off. Well, join the club.

I brush by him, and he grabs my arm. "I bought the coffee shop where you work."

I scrunch my brow, totally lost. "What?"

"Yeah. Now I'm your boss and it looks like favoritism to the other employees, so you should quit."

I yank my arm from his grip. "I worked there first. Besides, how can it be favoritism if we had a prior relationship?"

"Because I stepped into a position of authority."

I plant my hands on my hips. "I'm not quitting on your say-so."

"I could fire you."

I drop my hands. *Is he serious? Who is this man?* I thought I knew him. I thought he was a decent person. "You'd do that?"

He shakes his head. "I didn't buy the coffee shop. I wanted you to see how it could've been the other way."

I see red, fury flooding me. "Oh, so an intellectual exercise designed to scare the crap out of me after you've humiliated me. Thanks so much."

I walk away, head held high. I'm going to finish today's class if it kills me. Connor Rourke will not best me.

Just as I pull the door open, he says from behind me, "You're a coward."

I whirl. "You're a dick."

I walk away on shaky legs, trying desperately to hold off tears. I will get through this. I don't need someone like him in my life. I'm moving forward.

I'm strong, I'm determined, I'm...*devastated.*

18

———

Connor

I fucked up. First I was pissed off that she gave up on us and, once that faded, I was just very, very sad. I wanted to keep Becca in my life, and somehow I ruined everything. I crossed the line, said things I shouldn't have. If there was an instruction manual on how to make a relationship work, I'd be an example of what not to do. It's been three days and I still have no clue how to make it better. I can't possibly make things any worse. She won't talk to me, won't see me. I just want things to go back to the way they were. Class ends this Saturday, and I can't bear to think it's the last time I'm ever going to see her.

It's lunch break at work, and I join the crew and my brothers at our makeshift table, unwrapping my usual roast beef, provolone, and potato chip sandwich and stare at it. I have this same sandwich every day to save money. I'm always looking to the future, saving my money for some day, and now when I look to the future, all I see is a dark void without Becca.

"That sandwich needs some hot sauce," Jack says, gesturing to the hot sauce in the center of the table. It's not a prank. At least so far it hasn't been. Watch today be the day he's switched it up with something gross or scorching hot.

"No, thanks," I say flatly.

He shakes his head. "I thought you'd be in a better mood since the water tower cleared yesterday. You were so worked up about it before."

"Yeah, I'm glad." I can't put much enthusiasm into my voice. Everything sucks so bad. It is good news for us though. The tower didn't get landmark status, but after class discussion on my case study (based on our business), I saw some new ways to approach the problem. We agreed to keep the water tower with a fence around it to prevent kids from climbing on it and a fresh new paint job, erasing the graffiti and restoring it to the way it looked back in the day when it was a marine rope factory. We kept the history without the hazard, which was a win-win.

Just then, Jack leaps from his seat. "Ry, what're you doing here?"

His fiancée, Riley, walks in, beaming at him. "I thought I'd surprise you and meet you for lunch. I had a meeting in lower Manhattan and hopped on the ferry."

He hugs her, grins, and pulls her to join us. "My fiancée is here." They take a seat at the table, and he starts making introductions to the crew, all while handing Riley half his sandwich.

My chest aches watching the two of them so happy and comfortable with each other. I remember when Riley came to me, asking me to help arrange for her to show up at our worksite and win Jack back by showing him all the things she kept from their relationship, including an engraved brick with her future married name on it—Riley Walsh-Rourke. That engraved brick is now part of the pathway in our first development project. After her big symbolic gesture, she then declared her love for Jack in front of all of us. It took balls, and Jack didn't respond right away. Talk about putting your heart on the line. And now look at them so frigging happy together.

What am I doing sitting here wallowing in misery? I need to use my balls of steel and tell Becca the truth. I love her, I'll never stop loving her, and I'm willing to fight for us.

I stand. "I gotta go. Emergency. Tell Dylan I won't be back today."

"Hey, hey," Jack says. "As crew chief, I can't let you bail on work with no notice."

"I'm following Riley's brick example," I say.

She smiles. "Aww, he's going to tell her how much he loves her. Remember when I gave you that brick?"

He kisses her, waving me off. "Course I do, my beautiful loving fiancée."

I don't wait around for the rest of the mushy conversation. I've got my own stuff to deal with.

The whole subway ride I'm working on what I'm going to say. I know she's at the coffee shop Tuesday afternoons. I don't even know if she's still taking that job out in LA since she won't talk to me. I'm going to start with how I never should've crossed the line making an announcement to the class. It felt right at the time. She was floundering because of me, the class was nonresponsive because of her involvement with me, and it just seemed like the elephant in the room. I should've just ignored it and let it go. I could've gotten through the remaining classes. Yes, it was painful to watch her struggle, but that's my problem. She was trying and I should've let her do her thing.

When I get to the coffee shop, there's only a couple of people in line for coffee, so I wait for her to get their drink orders by the end of the counter.

The moment she notices me, she scowls. "I'm working."

"I know. I'll stay for your break and then we're going to talk." I lift a hand in greeting to her boss, Judy, a woman in her sixties with a lot of energy.

"Do what you want," Becca snaps. "I'm busy."

Judy shoots me a sympathetic look. Obviously Becca's not that busy since there's only a couple of people in here. She just doesn't want to see me. How did things get so screwed up? Those two customers leave and the whole place is dead. It's just after noon, not a real busy time since most people are getting lunch. They only offer breakfast-type foods here.

I decide I'll order a coffee and wait as long as it takes for her to talk to me. When she hands me my drink, I say, "I'll be waiting right over there for your break." I point to a table by the front window.

"I don't want to talk to you," she says through her teeth.

"Then you can listen. Please, Bec. Just hear me out and, if you still don't want to talk to me after I've said what I came here to say, then I'll leave you alone."

"I need to clean the machines," she says.

Judy pipes up. "Take your break, Becca. I got it."

Becca takes off her apron in jerky motions and walks out from behind the counter, gesturing toward a table in the corner.

I follow her there, taking the seat across from her. "I like your boss."

"Connor, why're you here?"

"Okay, first, I'm sorry. I said some things in the heat of the moment that I didn't mean. You're not a coward. I regret saying that *a lot*, and I crossed the line addressing the class. I was just trying to fix the problem, and I see now that it wasn't the way to go about it."

"No, it wasn't," she says quietly, staring at the table. "Do you have any idea how humiliating that was for me?" She lifts her head, her expression tight. "I still have to face those people on Saturday. I'm not sure how I got through the rest of class last Saturday."

"Because you're strong and determined. I should've kept my mouth shut. I lost my mind. I see us in a serious relationship. I thought you were on the same page, and then you went off with Simone for some new job far away, and I thought I was wrong about us. Am I wrong, Bec?"

Her lower lip wobbles, and she blinks rapidly. Maybe I am wrong. Maybe she's already made plans to move to LA. Desperation claws at my insides.

"Bec, I'm going to lay it out there, okay? From the beginning I was so caught up in you, I couldn't wait to be with you. It seemed impossible to wait four months. I don't regret a moment of our time together, except for the part where I hurt you. I never wanted that, and I swear I will never do anything like that again." I suck in air. "If you'll forgive me, we'll always be a team from here on out, and we'll work out a plan ahead of time to fix problems together."

Her chin quivers.

"Oh, shit. Don't cry. I take it back."

"You can't take it back! I love that plan. I love you!"

She stands, holding her arms out to me, and I don't hesitate, wrapping her in a tight hug. My eyes water. "I thought I lost you." I kiss her hair. "I'm so glad I didn't lose you."

She burrows into my chest. "I've been so miserable."

"Me too." I pull back to look at her. "What about the job with Simone?"

She wipes her eyes. "She changed her mind after seeing me meet some of the music industry guys. She says I'm not aggressive enough. No hard feelings. Can you believe that?"

I stroke her hair back from her face. "Yeah."

"But I have resting bitch face."

I smile a little. "I was not aware of that."

She nods, her sweet face determined on this matter. "My ex said I was an ice queen."

"You're anything but that. Honey, you cried the first time I told you I love you."

She sniffles. "I like honey better than babe. And I only cried because your eyes were so soulful and sincere, and your voice was so warm I felt it in my bones."

"God, it's been torture being apart. I didn't know if I'd ever get you back."

"I was so lost. I didn't know what to do. My plan blew up, and then I just was so mad I couldn't think straight."

I take a seat and pull her into my lap. "Yeah, not my finest moment, but I had noble intentions."

She rubs my chest. "Because of your royal blood?"

"Sure, let's go with that. It sounds better than I was desperate to fix everything so we'd be good again."

"Oh, Con, I really like your idea of being a team. Let's always check in with each other whenever there's a problem *before* one of us impulsively comes up with a solution. That way we're making decisions with good reasonable judgment instead of letting our emotions get the better of us."

I let out a breath of pure relief. She's back, we're on the same page, and we're working *with* each other instead of *against* each other. And she called me Con in her warm voice, not Connor. "So there's still the problem of you being out of a job."

"I know. It's not like any university would hire me now."

"Did you love teaching? I'm sure we could come up with some way for you to do it."

Her brows furrow. "You know what? I didn't love being in front of the classroom. I liked sharing what I know, but it was hard to see the results right away. Like at a work project you can see the results. Teaching, you usually don't see your students again after graduation, and you never know if you had an impact."

"You sure had an impact on me."

She laughs, and I soak in the beauty of a smiling, happy Becca. Happy with me. And then I have a great idea. I was part of the reason her job fell apart, and I can be the solution too. What good is being COO if I can't make the important decisions?

"Bec, work for my company. You love building projects, and you know management. You could help us with the management part of it. You've already studied us in class. I feel like you have a good handle of where we're at and where we need to go."

She sits straighter, her eyes lighting up. "I could be CSO."

I lower my voice to a husky tone. "Chief sexy officer, yeah, you are."

She laughs. "Chief strategy officer. Part creative thinker, part strategist. Reporting directly to the CEO, not you, though we'd work as a team. Do you think Dylan would want me on board?"

"I want you. I'll make it happen."

She smiles and cups my cheek. "Are you making up this position just to keep me close?"

"I legitimately think you'll make a great contribution to the business."

"Aww, thank you."

I give her a sexy smile. "And I want you in a personal, entirely workplace-inappropriate way."

"Con!"

"Hey, my brothers and I own the company, so it's perfectly fine."

She gives me a stern look. "We need to keep it professional at work."

I let that slide because, hey, sometimes insane chemistry can get out of control. "In any case, you're in on my say-so."

She worries her lower lip. "I should still bring my résumé and meet with Dylan."

"We'll discuss all the particulars ahead of time so you can wow him. You on board?"

She beams. "Yes."

"Great." I kiss her cheek and whisper in her ear, "Now can we please go back to your place for hot makeup sex?"

She smiles. "Yes. Only because you asked so politely." She stands. "Let me just ask my boss."

She crosses over to Judy to ask.

"Go," Judy says, giving me a wink. "I got this, lovebirds."

Becca leans over the counter to hug Judy and turns back to me with a bright smile. "Let's go, HBG."

I chuckle. Hot Builder Guy. I like it.

～

Becca

The moment I get Con inside my place, I launch myself at him. He catches me, wrapping his arms around me and walking me to my bedroom while I kiss him all over his scruffy face. I don't think he's shaved in days.

He sets me down next to the bed, and we rip each other's clothes off, mouths fused, crazed to be together again. We tumble into bed, a tangle of arms and legs.

"I love you," he says, kissing my neck.

I grab his head to gaze into his eyes. "I love *you*." I kiss him tenderly with all the feeling in my heart.

He smiles, and then he's kissing his way down my body, and I'm lit up inside. This is true love, and there's nothing holding us back anymore.

I tug at his hair, urging him up. "I can't wait."

He kisses me long and deep before grabbing a condom from the nightstand. And then he's back, thrusting deep inside me. He entwines our fingers, pressing my hands to the mattress as he rises over me.

"I love you so much," he says gruffly.

"Me too." I lift my hips. "More."

He smiles against my lips and then he gives me what I need, a hot, exhilarating heart-pumping ride. I'm panting, chanting his name, and then I'm right there, on the edge of release. He shifts my hips up with one large hand, changing the angle just right. I gasp as an explosion of pleasure rocks me to my core. He pumps hard and fast right along with me, bringing more and more pleasure. His lips press against my neck in a low groan as he lets go.

I hug him. "Wonderful man!"

His shoulders shake, and he lifts his head, smiling. "Wonderful, beautiful woman. Did I tell you that I love you?"

I beam. "Yes, you did, but I don't mind hearing it again."

"I love you so damn much."

"I love you too."

He kisses me and rolls to my side. We're quiet for a few moments, holding hands in the aftermath. I think back to all the time we were seeing each other in class, trying to hide our feelings from the world when everyone picked up on it anyway. I still think his company's case study was educational and worth spending time on. And I also think Con got something out of class too. Despite the fallout, I no longer believe my class was a total fail.

"Did you do your final paper?" I ask him.

He turns his head to look at me. "No. I thought I wasn't invited back to class."

"Do it. You have every right to be there, and it won't

change the outcome of class for me anyway. I want you to finish."

"Don't be a business school dropout, huh?"

"Exactly. Just no grand announcements this time, okay?"

"Bec, I swear I only spoke up out of desperation. I thought I'd lost you."

I roll on top of him, and he wraps his arms around me. "Well, you'll never have to worry about that again."

Becca

Con's back for our last class, and people seem more relaxed this time. Maybe because they've all turned in their final paper. Maybe because I showed them that I could deal with the situation and returned to class after my exit last Saturday in utter mortification. Maybe because I brought two platters of homemade Christmas cookies.

I nod encouragingly as Anita does her presentation on her paper's topic, which has to do with the buyout of her company by a larger one and the debilitating effect layoffs had on her and her remaining coworkers.

I take some satisfaction in listening to my influence on the presentations. I did teach them something. So far each of them has looked at their case study through the lens of change and how to work with it rather than fight it, longing for the old ways. It's an important lesson for the fast-paced business world. Change or die basically.

Class ends, and I actually feel a little emotional about it. "Before we go, I just want to thank you all for sharing your time with me. I know Saturday morning class isn't easy to get up for, but I do hope you got something out of it. I know I learned a lot listening to such smart dynamic businessmen and women. I look forward to hearing all you accomplish in the future. This is my last class. I've had a new business opportunity that I couldn't refuse, so it's on to the next part of my journey." I catch Con's eye, and he smiles warmly at me. I smile back, my heart filled to bursting. "Wishing every one of you all the best and happy holidays! Please take some cookies on your way out or I'll end up eating them all."

Everyone laughs and stops by the front to get a handful of cookies. Some say bye to me, some just say thanks for the cookies. I still don't know which woman filed a complaint against me, but I hope she's okay now. Nobody dropped out of class.

Con leaves without a goodbye, but I know he'll be waiting for me outside. He's still trying to be discreet to make sure the woman who felt uncomfortable with our relationship doesn't have to see it. He's a keeper.

The last person to go is Mike. To think I was so worried he'd be the problem just because he was so enthusiastic at my office hours and asked me out once.

"Take some cookies," I say to him. "There's still plenty."

He slowly turns to me. "Rebecca, I have a confession. I heard you got fired—"

"I wasn't fired. I was only here on a probationary basis, and I wasn't asked back. It all worked out fine."

He steps closer. "It was me who wrote a bad review on the teacher survey. After you turned me down, saying you never date a student, I realized you were seeing Connor. It was a low blow. Sorry it had such bad fallout."

I look away, unsure what to say. "Don't worry about it, Mike. You weren't the only one who left a poor review."

"That was me too."

My head whips toward him. "What do you mean?"

"I told everyone to give you bad reviews and I told them why. You had a favorite; you were inattentive and distracted; you didn't care about us."

I swallow hard. "But I did care."

"I turned them against you, and Carla sorta clinched the deal, telling everyone how she felt triggered. It was a pile on."

"I don't even know what to say to that."

"I do," a deep voice booms.

My hand flies to my throat and I whirl to face Dean Sears. He stalks forward, glowering down at Mike. "I heard every word. You'll be expelled for your part in defaming Ms.

Edwards's good character. Do you have any idea the damage you caused? We let her go, and her reputation in academia could've been destroyed, ending any future teaching opportunities. Serious career damage."

Mike lifts his chin. "You can't expel me. You have no proof."

Dean Sears crosses his arms. "I'm sure the other students will talk once I explain the consequences for falsely destroying a faculty member's reputation. Of course, I'll have to let your employer know they'll no longer need to cover your tuition."

Mike jabs a finger at me. "She's the one who was seeing a student! That's against university policy."

"It's over, Mike," I say quietly. "I'm no longer working here. Maybe next time you'll think about the consequences of your actions before you act out of spite."

His eyes narrow menacingly, and adrenaline spikes through me. Dean Sears moves quickly in front of me, blocking Mike from getting any closer. Mike lunges, upending both platters of cookies. They go flying everywhere. Then he stalks out the door, slapping the doorframe on his way out.

I take a few shaky breaths, my heart slowly going back to its normal rate. I can hardly believe what I just heard. That means only Carla and Mike had an issue with me, and Mike's complaint was completely unjustified. I wasn't such a horrible teacher after all. A huge weight lifts from my shoulders.

Dean Sears bends to pick up the cookies and I join him. "Rebecca, I'm sorry for this horrible misunderstanding. The evidence was damning, but I should've known you couldn't have been as terrible as those student reviews said. I regret not digging deeper."

I shake my head. "You were just doing your job. I have to take responsibility, too, for continuing to see Connor. I ignored the policy because I felt he was the exception. I was too upset at our meeting before to explain it well, but I was involved with him before class even began, he was auditing the class and not officially enrolled as a student, and it was completely consensual. I love him." It's as simple and wonderful as that.

He nods once. We finish picking up the cookie fragments in silence.

After we dump them in a nearby garbage can, he turns to me. "If you need a reference for another teaching job, I'm happy to give one."

I smile. "Thanks, but I have a new opportunity that I'm very excited about. I'm just pleased that my students actually did get something useful from my class."

He inclines his head. "Happy holidays, Rebecca. Send my love to your parents."

"I will. You too!"

He leaves and I return to the lectern, standing there for a moment, soaking in a last look at my classroom. Even though I don't plan to stick with teaching, it means so much to me to know my students didn't hate my class. I think it was a worthy class. I can hold my head high around my parents—two fabulous teachers—and feel like I did the best I could, and my best wasn't so bad after all.

I let out a long breath, smile, and head out the door for the next part of the rest of my life with Con.

EPILOGUE

Regency Christmas ball in Villroy

Connor

I can't believe I'm wearing breeches. With stockings too! My cousin's wife, Alice, says all of us guys look "dashing" in our Regency formal wear. Alice is an American, but she loves the Regency era of England. This is all her wacky idea, putting the men in black coats with tails, white shirts with something called a cravat knotted at the neck, tan breeches, and white stockings. At least I'm wearing my own dress shoes.

"It's like a fairy tale," Becca whispers in awe as she looks around the palace ballroom. It is an impressive room, an enormous space with multiple crystal and gold chandeliers, frescoed ceiling paintings, and glossy inlaid wooden floors. The Christmas greenery and abundance of glowing candles take it to another level, making it feel both grand and warmly festive.

My irritation fades. I mostly agreed to spend Christmas on Villroy to indulge Becca's fascination with my royal side. Honestly, the Regency-style dress she's wearing—a pale blue with short sleeves that exposes her cleavage and falls in a silky cascade from its high waist to her ankles—really suits her. She looks incredibly beautiful. And I'm not just saying that because I'm crazy in love with her.

Alice rushes over to us in a Regency dress similar to Becca's but bright pink, her blond hair up in a bun with two ringlets of hair framing her face. "Oh my gosh, Becca! You look fabulous! Are your ancestors from England?"

Becca flushes pink. "Some of them. And thank you. You look wonderful too."

Alice's eyes are wide behind her cat's-eye glasses with hearts on the sides. "You look like an English rose! Truly. Can I take your picture? You're inspiring me so much. I might put you in my next book with your fair complexion, flaxen locks, and swanlike neck."

Becca darts a nervous look toward me.

I grin. "Are you gonna make her the heroine of your next Regency romance? Because maybe I should be the hero." I wink at Becca, who leans against my side, smiling. The woman is just as crazy about me as I am about her.

Alice pulls her phone from a tiny purse and snaps a picture of us.

"Do you read romance?" Alice asks Becca, tucking her phone away.

"No. I mostly read literary novels."

Alice smiles brightly, unperturbed. "Well, if you ever want something fun to read, let me know and I'll make some recommendations or give you one of mine."

"Okay, thank you," Becca says politely.

Alice fills us in on some background history completely unprovoked. "Christmas in Regency England was technically celebrated over twelve days from December twenty-fifth to January sixth, the festival of the Epiphany. That's what they're referring to in the 'Twelve Days of Christmas' song. I bended the rules a bit to suit our schedule, having it a little earlier."

"Connor bends the rules too," Becca says with a smile. She claims I said that was my rationale for dating her when she was my teacher—bending the rules to suit myself. Truth is, I couldn't resist her and she knows it. So maybe I did bend the rules, but can you blame me? I couldn't let her slip away.

"Fellow rebel, all right!" Alice gives me a high five.

My cousin Lucas approaches in his black Regency formal wear. It's the same outfit all of us men are wearing, but it looks more natural on him than on me and my brothers, probably because he grew up in a more formal environment here at the palace. "There you are," he croons to Alice in his unique Villroy accent. It's formal English with a hint of French cadence, since Villroy is right off the coast of southwestern France. He pulls Alice close and kisses her before turning to us. "Well, what do you think of the ball?"

"It's amazing!" Becca exclaims. "The ballroom alone would be enough to dazzle, but then you add in the Christmas decorations with the greenery and all the candles and mirrors. It's breathtaking."

Alice beams. "We added mirrors to reflect the candlelight. We also have kissing boughs made of evergreens, mistletoe, and apples." She points out the green globes hanging from the ceiling. "Make sure you stand under one."

"We tested them all out," Lucas says proudly. "All of them work splendidly."

"Oh, you," Alice says affectionately.

The band starts playing and Lucas executes a formal bow. "May I have the pleasure of this dance, Lady Alice?"

She curtsies. "Yes, you may, my prince." She takes his arm and turns to us. "You guys should join us. It's a Regency country dance, very simple to follow along. Later, we're going to waltz and attempt a Scottish reel."

I turn to Becca in question. She bites her lower lip, looking uncomfortable. I've never danced with her besides at that club for Simone's birthday party. This is a very different style of dancing.

"We're going to get refreshments first," I say.

"Good idea," Alice says. "The dance lasts an hour before there's a break."

"Just lemonade for you, my beautiful wife." Lucas turns to us and smiles. "She's newly pregnant."

"Congratulations," Becca and I say in near unison.

Alice beams. "Thank you. Make sure you try the eggnog. It's authentic!"

The two of them join a long line of dancers moving energetically around each other. It's mostly my cousins, their wives, and some relatives I don't know. Even my parents are out there.

Becca takes my hand and we head over to a long refreshment table at the side of the ballroom. "I'd much prefer lemonade." She makes a disgusted face, screwing up her nose and sticking her tongue out. "Eggnog, yuck."

I grin. "Too bad they don't serve beer at Regency balls."

I pour us both a glass of lemonade from the crystal pitcher, and we watch the dancers.

Brendan appears at our side, helping himself to a glass of red punch. "I have it on good authority the punch is spiked with rum and brandy." He takes a sip and grins. "Actually, this is my second cup and I'm feeling it. Apparently, they don't serve food at a Regency ball."

"Didn't you hear Anna announce there'd be a formal dinner at eleven?" I ask. Anna is the queen of Villroy, my cousin Gabriel's wife.

"I missed it. I was running late. Jet lag caught up with me, and I slept longer than I meant to." He lifts his glass and lowers it, staring across the room. "Who is that redhead? Please tell me we're not related."

I glance over at a young red-haired woman watching the dancing from the other side of the ballroom. Brendan has a thing for redheads, thinks they're more fiery, but she doesn't look fiery to me. She looks thoughtful like she's a million miles away instead of standing in a green Regency dress at a noisy palace ball.

"She must be connected to someone in the royal family if she's here," I point out.

"I'm going to ask her to dance," Brendan says, handing me his drink.

"Sure, I'll hold your drink," I say dryly. "Just call me the butler."

A large palace guard—wearing the unmistakable uniform of black blazer, black T-shirt, and black trousers—gets to the red-haired woman first, and she follows him out the door.

Brendan returns and takes back his drink. "Did you see that? She has her own palace guard."

"Then she must be royal," I say. "And probably related somehow."

"Damn," he mutters.

My brothers wander over to the refreshment table with us —Sean, Jack, and Beast. They look as uncomfortable in their Regency formal wear as I feel. Beast can't even button his topcoat because his shoulders are too bulky with muscle, stretching the seams of the coat. Any minute now he's going to bust out of it.

"How'd you two get out of dancing?" I ask, waving my finger at Sean and Jack. "I was sure your women would have you out there doing the country line dance or whatever it's called."

"They're getting a tour with Anna," Sean says, pulling at his cravat. "Temporary reprieve."

"I like dancing," Jack says, pouring himself some lemonade. "No problem for me."

"Do you like this kind of dancing?" I ask Becca.

She glances at the dance floor, where the dancers are weaving in and out of each other. "It seems like everyone knows the rules to that dance. I'm more of a freeform dancer. You know." She does a cute hip swivel. Frigging adorable. I pull her close and kiss her hair.

We stand around, sipping our drinks, watching the action until Anna arrives—Queen Anna—with a breathless Josie and a wide-eyed Riley. Josie's in a bright yellow gown, Riley in a purplish-pink, and Anna in a white gown that shows off her round pregnant belly. She's due in February, a boy this time who she confided will be named Leo, though we have to keep it on the down low because Gabriel follows the royal protocol of announcing the name formally to the public when the child is born.

"We saw the audience chamber," Josie gushes. "Double hand-carved wooden thrones!"

"We sat on them too," Riley says. "Can you believe it? We were like Queen One and Queen Two."

The three women crack up.

Once she calms down enough to talk, Josie goes on. "And we also saw the parlor, the courtyard, and the formal dining room."

"We're going to have dinner there tonight!" Riley exclaims. She's usually pretty mellow, so it must've made a big impression.

Anna beams at them. She's young with dark brown curly hair and bright brown eyes. "I love your enthusiasm. The palace had a similar effect on me the first time I saw it." She's an American too. I guess us Americans aren't used to grand royal palaces.

"Hey, Anna," Brendan says and then corrects himself. "I mean, Your Majesty Highness Queen Anna."

Anna bursts out laughing. "We're family. Please just call me Anna." It's supposed to be "Your Majesty" for the king and queen. It's the princes and princesses who are "Your Highness." Hmm, maybe I can get Becca to call me that while we're here. Ha-ha.

Brendan inclines his head. "Anna, sure. Earlier I saw a woman in her twenties standing on the side of the ballroom. Red hair, green dress. Who is it?"

Anna thinks for a moment. "Red hair was probably Chloe. Did she look like she was thinking hard, a million miles away?"

"I dunno," Brendan says. "She was just standing there."

"Yeah," I put in. "She looked thoughtful, completely unaware of the dancers and the noise."

Anna nods. "Yup, that's Chloe. She's your cousin Adrian's wife's sister. She's from Brooklyn too, though she lives in Manhattan now."

"So not a relative," Brendan says with a wide smile. "But why does she need a guard?"

"She doesn't." Anna signals, and a servant brings her a glass of water.

Becca shoots me a sideways glance that says exactly what I'm thinking—must be nice to have servants do your bidding.

Brendan presses on. "I saw Chloe leave with a guard."

"Oh, that's Michael." Anna lowers her voice. "He doesn't guard her. They're, well, I'm not sure what they are. It's complicated."

"Huh," Brendan says.

"It's kinda sweet, isn't it?" Josie asks. "Falling for your bodyguard."

Sean clears his throat loudly.

Josie hugs him around his middle, smiling up at him. "You're the only bodyguard I'd ever fall for."

"Damn right," he grumbles.

Since when is Sean a bodyguard? I glance at my brothers for confirmation, but the only one paying attention is Beast, who rolls his eyes. Must be an inside joke between Sean and Josie.

"He's not her bodyguard." Anna smiles at the servant who just presented her with a glass of water, murmurs thank you, and takes a long swallow. The servant bows and walks away. "They just met here on Villroy when Chloe was visiting her sister. He was off duty at the time."

She finishes her water and sets it on a nearby table. Another servant whisks it away a moment later.

My cousin, King Gabriel, arrives holding his young daughter's hand. Mila is two years old with dark brown curly hair like her mom. Her hair is up in a messy bun with lots of loose curls hanging down, and she's wearing a cute red dress with ruffles. Gabriel gives us all a quick hello before turning to his wife, Anna. "I told her it was time to get ready for bed, but she wants to dance with Pop-Pop." It's kinda funny to hear him say "Pop-Pop" in his formal English. I'm sure my dad would love to dance with his honorary granddaughter.

Anna scoops Mila up and settles her on her hip. "Pop-Pop is dancing with Grandmom Tara."

Mila sticks her thumb in her mouth and leans against her

mom's shoulder for a second, but then she lifts her head again. "No bed."

Anna looks to Gabriel. "It is a special occasion."

He strokes Mila's hair out of her face. "You know how she gets when she hasn't had her sleep."

Anna sighs and turns to Mila. "Okay, my dear. You can do three spins with Pop-Pop, three spins with Grandmom Tara, and then it's bath and bedtime." She sets her down, and Mila races to the dance floor.

Gabriel chases after her, quickly directing her toward the edges so she won't get knocked over by the dancing adults.

Anna grins. "She's fearless just like a future queen should be." She turns at the sound of a woman calling her name. "Speaking of, Queen Polly, get over here, girl!"

It's my cousin Oscar and his wife, Polly. They're king and queen of her kingdom, Beaumont, a chain of islands in the Caribbean. Oscar went from a prince to a king. Not a bad upgrade. Polly's holding her baby girl against her chest.

A few moments later, they join us. Polly has dark brown curly hair and resembles Anna a bit, even though they're only very distantly related. She rubs the baby's back through a pink blanket. "She spit up a little, so I had to get rid of the burp rag. Do I smell okay?"

Anna sniffs her. "You smell of baby powder and new mom anxiety."

Becca takes a peek at the baby. "She's so cute. What's her name?"

Polly smiles down at her daughter. "This little four-month-old angel is Juliette, future queen of Beaumont."

"Wow, so many queens in one room," Becca says.

"And so many babies too," Anna exclaims. "Either cooking in the oven or fresh baked. Adrian and Sara have a three-month-old, Henry, too. They didn't want to bring him into this cesspool of germs. Adrian's words." She rolls her eyes. "He's such an overprotective dad. You'll see them on Christmas Eve when it's a little quieter. Alice is newly pregnant, and Emma just announced her pregnancy last month. Emma is five months along, but you can barely tell." She points out my cousin Emma sitting in a chair on the side of the room. Her husband, rock star Jackson Walker, stands next to her with a stern expression like he's her guard. Now that's overprotective. The baby's not even here yet.

"What a lovely family you have," Becca says.

"Thank you," Anna says. "I love 'em to pieces." Her eyes tear up. "Sorry, baby hormones make me extra emotional." She holds up a palm to a rapidly approaching Gabriel. "I'm fine."

He pulls her aside, speaking in a low voice. A few moments later, she says her goodbyes, and they collect Mila, who's cuddled on my mom's chest, twirling one of her curly locks of hair, thumb in her mouth.

After they leave, Becca looks up at me. "Now what, Prince Connor? Did you want to attempt this dance?"

"I've got a better idea. Let's go back to our room and take off these costumes."

"Con! I like my dress."

"Okay, three spins around and then it's bedtime." I give her my sexiest smile.

She laughs. "Angel, more like devil." She kisses me. "A quick break in our room *after* we slow dance. I have to be back in time for the formal dinner in the royal dining room."

I pinch her chin. "What a tough negotiator. Okay, we'll slow dance first. And then I can't wait to get you back to the room. I've got an early Christmas gift I want to give you in private."

She eyes me suspiciously, and I laugh. "For real. I swear on my sister's life."

She shakes her head, laughing. She knows I don't have a sister.

~

Becca

The ball was a lot of fun once the music changed to a waltz. Of course neither of us knew how to waltz, so we just did a slow sway to beautiful music in a grand ballroom.

Then we made a getaway for some alone time in our room. I would normally not miss a moment of any of this—I mean, how often do I attend a ball in a royal palace?—but Con said he wanted to give me my Christmas gift early. He wants it to be just the two of us, not a crowd on Christmas morning. I'm excited. I'm pretty sure it's legit, and he's not just trying to seduce me. Though, if he did try, I know I'd melt. The sexual tension's been building over the past two days since we've hardly been alone or awake enough to do anything about it.

The moment we're alone in our room, he pulls me into his arms and kisses me. Suddenly we're crazed for each other. It's wild and hot and I love it. Next thing I know, we're naked in the giant four-poster bed, joined as close as two people can be, and he's taking me higher and higher. I go off like a firecracker, only dimly aware of his own groan as he lets go.

He gives me his weight, and I wrap my arms around him in a tight hug. My prince, my fantastic lover, my hot builder guy. He's everything I ever wanted and never thought to look for in my dating app. I didn't think a man like him existed. I'm the luckiest woman on Earth.

Long moments later, he lifts his head. "Be right back."

He disappears into the bathroom, and I lounge on the bed, completely relaxed. I hope the Regency costumes aren't too wrinkled lying on the floor somewhere.

He returns, pulls on his boxer briefs, and goes to his suitcase, taking out a shiny red wrapped gift with a bow on top. He gets in bed with me, lying on his side, and hands it to me.

I clap and sit up. "I almost forgot. I'll get yours too."

He holds me in place with a hand on my shoulder. "Open yours first."

"Same time?"

His voice is tender, his gaze soft. "No, love, it has to be you."

My breath hitches, my heart thumping hard. "Why?"

His blue eyes twinkle. He definitely got me something good. "Because."

I carefully remove the paper with shaking hands. Oh,

wow. It's a beautiful maple wood jewelry box. "Con, it's *gorgeous*."

"I made it for you."

I stare at him in awe. My hot builder guy made this with his own two capable hands. *Swoon!* "I love it so much! Oh, Con, the craftsmanship is just divine." I stare at it and then lift my gaze to his. "I think I have to get you another present."

He smiles. "I'm sure I'll love whatever you picked out. Open your jewelry box. There's a key." He points to where he taped a small metal key on the bottom.

I unlock it and a secret compartment drawer on the side pops open. I gasp. "A secret drawer!" I slide it open to find a blue velvet pouch. I open it and pull out a diamond ring. "Oh my God." I can't believe this. A beautifully made jewelry box with a secret drawer *and* a diamond ring. All I got him was one little thing I didn't even make.

"Con…" I trail off. He's on one knee by the side of the bed.

I clap a hand over my mouth. I was so enthralled with the secret drawer I didn't put it together at first.

"Becca, I fell in love with you the very first time we met, and I've only been falling deeper and deeper with each passing day. Will you spend the rest of your life with me and be my wife?"

"Yes!"

He rises smoothly to his feet, pulls me out of bed, and hugs me tight. Tears spill out as the shock wears off. I'm just so happy.

He cradles my face with both hands. "Your plan worked, Bec. Settled by thirty."

"I'm not thirty until April," I manage over the lump in my throat.

He smiles and kisses me. "So we're a little ahead of schedule. You like that."

"I do." I wipe tears away with a laugh. "Look at me already saying 'I do.' I can't top your gift, but let me get it anyway." I grab the sheet, wrapping it around me for warmth, and fetch the small box from my suitcase.

I bite my lower lip and hand it to him. "It's no ring, but…"

He rips the paper off and opens it. "My own key. Thank you."

"I was going to ask you to move in with me. My place is bigger and you seemed comfortable there. Would you like that?"

"I'd love that. I should've opened your gift first like you said. Then mine would've been the icing on top."

I throw my arms around him, and my sheet drops to the floor. "Yours is the cake, the icing, and all the decorations."

He laughs.

I stare at my new ring. "Only, if anyone asks, I'm not going to say you proposed to me when we were naked in bed. It sounds like it was in the heat of the moment instead of, you know, devastatingly romantic."

He draws me back into bed and pulls the covers over us, lying side by side. "It wasn't the heat of the moment. I've been wanting this for a while now. Besides, who would ask?"

I rub his chest and admire my sparkly diamond ring at the same time. "Everyone always wants to know how the guy proposed."

"They do?"

"Yes, women talk."

"You want me to ask you again?"

I tear my gaze away from my sparkly ring and meet his eyes. "Would you?"

"Sure, honey. Guess how I'm going to do it?"

I think for a moment. "Oh! You're going to wait until Christmas Eve, draw me over to the mistletoe, kiss me, and then go down on one knee."

"That's exactly what I planned to do."

"It is?"

He laughs. "No, you just told me what you really want."

"It's a good plan. Make sure we're alone though. It's private."

"That might be harder to arrange. Let's do it now."

My brow furrows, trying to imagine it. "You want me to

get dressed and wander through the drafty palace in search of mistletoe?"

"No, I want you to stay naked in bed." He pulls me close, nuzzling into my neck, his hands roaming everywhere. No way I'm leaving this bed. He kisses along my jaw to the sensitive spot behind my ear. "Let's just *say* we did all that Christmas Eve stuff and enjoy our sexier engagement right here." He kisses me deeply, and I'm lost. This man. This wonderful man.

When he finally lets me up for air, I say, "You're impossible to resist!"

He rolls on top of me and grins. "I know."

Don't miss the next book in the series *Rogue Devil*, featuring Brendan in a slow burn friends-to-lovers romance!

Chloe

Friends with benefits isn't a real thing. Nope. Once you cross the line, that friendship is over. Ask me how I know. So I'm keeping my head down, focused on getting into medical school and ultimately working to find the cure for cancer. I want my life to mean something, to give back something significant to the world. Guys are a distraction I can't afford.

Brendan

From the moment I met Chloe Travers, a protective streak I never knew I had took over. Despite my raging lust, I kept her at arm's length. We have a family connection, which means casually hooking up is out. Too much potential fallout and awkward future encounters.

And then she moves in next door for the summer. Awkward? More like the ultimate test of my willpower. We're spending every spare moment together as friends, and it's driving me insane. I want to cross that line, but what if I make a move and lose her?

Sign up for my newsletter to be emailed when *Rogue Devil* releases at kyliegilmore.com/newsletter

ALSO BY KYLIE GILMORE

Happy Endings Book Club Series <<the Campbell family and a romance book club collide!

Hidden Hollywood (Book 1)

Inviting Trouble (Book 2)

So Revealing (Book 3)

Formal Arrangement (Book 4)

Bad Boy Done Wrong (Book 5)

Mess With Me (Book 6)

Resisting Fate (Book 7)

Chance of Romance (Book 8)

Wicked Flirt (Book 9)

An Inconvenient Plan (Book 10)

A Happy Endings Wedding (Book 11)

The Clover Park Series <<brothers who put family first!

The Opposite of Wild (Book 1)

Daisy Does It All (Book 2)

Bad Taste in Men (Book 3)

Kissing Santa (Book 4)

Restless Harmony (Book 5)

Not My Romeo (Book 6)

Rev Me Up (Book 7)

An Ambitious Engagement (Book 8)

Clutch Player (Book 9)

A Tempting Friendship (Book 10)

Clover Park Bride: Nico and Lily's Wedding

A Valentine's Day Gift (Book 11)

Maggie Meets Her Match (Book 12)

The Clover Park STUDS series <<hawt geeks who unleash into studs!

Almost Over It (Book 1)

Almost Married (Book 2)

Almost Fate (Book 3)

Almost in Love (Book 4)

Almost Romance (Book 5)

Almost Hitched (Book 6)

The Rourkes Series <<swoonworthy princes and kickass princesses!

Royal Catch (Book 1)

Royal Hottie (Book 2)

Royal Darling (Book 3)

Royal Charmer (Book 4)

Royal Player (Book 5)

Royal Shark (Book 6)

Rogue Prince (Book 7)

Rogue Gentleman (Book 8)

Rogue Rascal (Book 9)

Rogue Angel (Book 10)

Rogue Devil (Book 11)

Rogue Beast (Book 12)

ABOUT THE AUTHOR

Kylie Gilmore is the *USA Today* bestselling author of The Rourkes series, the Happy Endings Book Club series, the Clover Park series, and the Clover Park STUDS series. She writes humorous romance that makes you laugh, cry, and reach for a cold glass of water.

Kylie lives in New York with her family, two cats, and a nutso dog. When she's not writing, wrangling kids, or dutifully taking notes at writing conferences, you can find her flexing her muscles all the way to the high cabinet for her secret chocolate stash.

Sign up for Kylie's Newsletter and get a FREE book! kyliegilmore.com/newsletter

For more fun stuff check out Kylie's website https://www.kyliegilmore.com.

Thanks for reading *Rogue Angel.* I hope you enjoyed it. Would you like to know about new releases? You can sign up for my new release email list at kyliegilmore.com/newsletter. I promise not to clog your inbox! Only new release info, sales, and some fun giveaways.

I love to hear from readers! You can find me at:
   kyliegilmore.com
   Instagram.com/kyliegilmore
   Facebook.com/KylieGilmoreToo
   Twitter @KylieGilmoreToo

If you liked Connor and Becca's story, please leave a review on your favorite retailer's website or Goodreads. Thank you.